At Fault

At Fault
Kate Chopin

MINT EDITIONS

At Fault was first published in 1890.

This edition published by Mint Editions 2021.

ISBN 9781513271606 | E-ISBN 9781513276601

Published by Mint Editions®

MINT
EDITIONS

minteditionbooks.com

Publishing Director: Jennifer Newens
Design & Production: Rachel Lopez Metzger
Project Manager: Micaela Clark
Typesetting: Westchester Publishing Services

Contents

I

The Mistress of Place-du-Bois

When Jérôme Lafirme died, his neighbors awaited the results of his sudden taking off with indolent watchfulness. It was a matter of unusual interest to them that a plantation of four thousand acres had been left unincumbered to the disposal of a handsome, inconsolable, childless Creole widow of thirty. A *bêtise* of some sort might safely be looked for. But time passing, the anticipated folly failed to reveal itself; and the only wonder was that Thérèse Lafirme so successfully followed the methods of her departed husband.

Of course Thérèse had wanted to die with her Jérôme, feeling that life without him held nothing that could reconcile her to its further endurance. For days she lived alone with her grief; shutting out the appeals that came to her from the demoralized "hands," and unmindful of the disorder that gathered about her. Till Uncle Hiram came one day with a respectful tender of sympathy, offered in the guise of a reckless misquoting of Scripture—and with a grievance.

"Mistuss," he said, "I 'lowed 'twar best to come to de house an' tell you; fur Massa he alluz did say 'Hi'urm, I counts on you to keep a eye open endurin' my appersunce;' you ricollic, marm?" addressing an expanse of black bordered cambric that veiled the features of his mistress. "Things is a goin' wrong; dat dey is. I don't wants to name no names 'doubt I'se 'bleeged to; but dey done start a kiarrin' de cotton seed off de place, and dats how."

If Hiram's information had confined itself to the bare statement of things "goin' wrong," such intimation, of its nature vague and susceptible of uncertain interpretation, might have failed to rouse Thérèse from her lethargy of grief. But that wrong doing presented as a tangible abuse and defiance of authority, served to move her to action. She felt at once the weight and sacredness of a trust, whose acceptance brought consolation and awakened unsuspected powers of doing.

In spite of Uncle Hiram's parting prediction "de cotton'll be a goin' naxt" no more seed was hauled under cover of darkness from Place-du-Bois.

The short length of this Louisiana plantation stretched along Cane River, meeting the water when that stream was at its highest, with a thick growth of cotton-wood trees; save where a narrow convenient opening had been cut into their midst, and where further down the pine hills started in abrupt prominence from the water and the dead level of land on either side of them. These hills extended in a long line of gradual descent far back to the wooded borders of Lac du Bois; and within the circuit which they formed on the one side, and the irregular half circle of a sluggish bayou on the other, lay the cultivated open ground of the plantation—rich in its exhaustless powers of reproduction.

Among changes which the railroad brought soon after Jérôme Lafirme's death, and which were viewed by many as of questionable benefit, was one which drove Thérèse to seek another domicile. The old homestead that nestled to the hill side and close to the water's edge, had been abandoned to the inroads of progressive civilization; and Mrs. Lafirme had rebuilt many rods away from the river and beyond sight of the mutilated dwelling, converted now into a section house. In building, she avoided the temptations offered by modern architectural innovations, and clung to the simplicity of large rooms and broad verandas: a style whose merits had stood the test of easy-going and comfort-loving generations.

The negro quarters were scattered at wide intervals over the land, breaking with picturesque irregularity into the systematic division of field from field; and in the early spring-time gleaming in their new coat of whitewash against the tender green of the sprouting cotton and corn.

Thérèse loved to walk the length of the wide verandas, armed with her field-glass, and to view her surrounding possessions with comfortable satisfaction. Then her gaze swept from cabin to cabin; from patch to patch; up to the pine-capped hills, and down to the station which squatted a brown and ugly intruder within her fair domain.

She had made pouting resistance to this change at first, opposing it step by step with a conservatism that yielded only to the resistless. She pictured a visionary troop of evils coming in the wake of the railroad, which, in her eyes no conceivable benefits could mitigate. The occasional tramp, she foresaw as an army; and the travelers whom chance deposited at the store that adjoined the station, she dreaded as an endless procession of intruders forcing themselves upon her privacy.

Grégoire, the young nephew of Mrs. Lafirme, whose duty on the plantation was comprehended in doing as he was bid, qualified by a propensity for doing as he liked, rode up from the store one day in the reckless fashion peculiar to Southern youth, breathless with the information that a stranger was there wishing audience with her.

Thérèse at once bristled with objections. Here was a confirmation of her worst dread. But encouraged by Grégoire's reiteration "he 'pear to me like a nice sort o' person," she yielded a grudging assent to the interview.

She sat within the wide hall-way beyond the glare and heat that were beating mercilessly down upon the world out of doors, engaged in a light work not so exacting as to keep her thoughts and glance from wandering. Looking through the wide open back doors, the picture which she saw was a section of the perfect lawn that encircled the house for an acre around, and from which Hiram was slowly raking the leaves cast from a clump of tall magnolias. Beneath the spreading shade of an umbrella-China tree, lay the burly Hector, but half awake to the possible nearness of tramps; and Betsy, a piece of youthful ebony in blue cottonade, was crossing leisurely on her way to the poultry yard; unheeding the scorching sun-rays that she thought were sufficiently parried by the pan of chick feed that she balanced adroitly on her bushy black head.

At the front, the view at certain seasons would have been clear and unbroken: to the station, the store, and out-lying hills. But now she could see beyond the lawn only a quivering curtain of rich green which the growing corn spread before the level landscape, and above whose swaying heads appeared occasionally the top of an advancing white sun-shade.

Thérèse was of a roundness of figure suggesting a future of excessive fullness if not judiciously guarded; and she was fair, with a warm whiteness that a passing thought could deepen into color. The waving blonde hair, gathered in an abundant coil on top of her head, grew away with a pretty sweep from the temples, the low forehead and nape of the white neck that showed above a frill of soft lace. Her eyes were blue, as certain gems are; that deep blue that lights, and glows, and tells things of the soul. When David Hosmer presented himself, they were intense only with expectancy and the color was in her cheek like the blush in a shell.

He was a tall individual of perhaps forty; thin and sallow. His black hair was streaked abundantly with grey, and his face marked with premature lines; left there by care, no doubt, and, by a too close attention to what men are pleased to call the main chances of life.

"A serious one," was Thérèse's first thought in looking at him. "A man who has never learned to laugh or who has forgotten how." Though plainly feeling the effects of the heat, he did not seem to appreciate the relief offered by the grateful change into this shadowy, sweet smelling, cool retreat; used as he was to ignore the comforting things of life when presented to him as irrelevant to that dominant main chance. He accepted under protest a glass of ice water from the wide-eyed Betsy, and suffered a fan to be thrust into his hand, seemingly to save his time or his timidity by its possibly unheeded rejection.

"Lor'-zee folks," exclaimed the observant Betsy on re-entering the kitchen, "dey'se a man in yonda, look like he gwine eat somebody up. I was fur gittin' 'way quick me."

It can be readily imagined that Hosmer lost little time in preliminary small talk. He introduced himself vaguely as from the West; then perceiving the need of being more specific as from Saint Louis. She had guessed he was no Southerner. He had come to Mrs. Lafirme on the part of himself and others with a moneyed offer for the privilege of cutting timber from her land for a given number of years. The amount named was alluring, but here was proposed another change and she felt plainly called on for resistance.

The company which he represented had in view the erection of a sawmill some two miles back in the woods, close beside the bayou and at a convenient distance from the lake. He was not wordy, nor was he eager in urging his plans; only in a quiet way insistent in showing points to be considered in her own favor which she would be likely herself to overlook.

Mrs. Lafirme, a clever enough business woman, was moved by no undue haste to give her answer. She begged for time to think the matter over, which Hosmer readily agreed to; expressing a hope that a favorable answer be sent to him at Natchitoches, where he would await her convenience. Then resisting rather than declining all further hospitality, he again took his way through the scorching fields.

Thérèse wanted but time to become familiar with this further change. Alone she went out to her beloved woods, and at the hush of mid-day, bade a tearful farewell to the silence.

II

AT THE MILL

David Hosmer sat alone in his little office of roughly fashioned pine board. So small a place, that with his desk and his clerk's desk, a narrow bed in one corner, and two chairs, there was scant room for a man to more than turn himself comfortably about. He had just dispatched his clerk with the daily bundle of letters to the post-office, two miles away in the Lafirme store, and he now turned with the air of a man who had well earned his moment of leisure, to the questionable relaxation of adding columns and columns of figures.

The mill's unceasing buzz made pleasant music to his ears and stirred reflections of a most agreeable nature. A year had gone by since Mrs. Lafirme had consented to Hosmer's proposal; and already the business more than gave promise of justifying the venture. Orders came in from the North and West more rapidly than they could be filled. That "Cypresse Funerall" which stands in grim majesty through the dense forests of Louisiana had already won its just recognition; and Hosmer's appreciation of a successful business venture was showing itself in a little more pronounced stoop of shoulder, a deepening of pre-occupation and a few additional lines about mouth and forehead.

Hardly had the clerk gone with his letters than a light footstep sounded on the narrow porch; the quick tap of a parasol was heard on the door-sill; a pleasant voice asking, "Any admission except on business?" and Thérèse crossed the small room and seated herself beside Hosmer's desk before giving him time to arise.

She laid her hand and arm,—bare to the elbow—across his work, and said, looking at him reproachfully:—

"Is this the way you keep a promise?"

"A promise?" he questioned, smiling awkwardly and looking furtively at the white arm, then very earnestly at the ink-stand beyond.

"Yes. Didn't you promise to do no work after five o'clock?"

"But this is merely pastime," he said, touching the paper, yet leaving it undisturbed beneath the fair weight that was pressing it down. "My work is finished: you must have met Henry with the letters."

"No, I suppose he went through the woods; we came on the hand-car. Oh, dear! It's an ungrateful task, this one of reform," and she leaned back, fanning leisurely, whilst he proceeded to throw the contents of his desk into hopeless disorder by pretended efforts at arrangement.

"My husband used sometimes to say, and no doubt with reason," she continued, "that in my eagerness for the rest of mankind to do right, I was often in danger of losing sight of such necessity for myself."

"Oh, there could be no fear of that," said Hosmer with a short laugh. There was no further pretext for continued occupation with his pens and pencils and rulers, so he turned towards Thérèse, rested an arm on the desk, pulled absently at his black moustache, and crossing his knee, gazed with deep concern at the toe of his boot, and set of his trouser about the ankle.

"You are not what my friend Homeyer would call an individualist," he ventured, "since you don't grant a man the right to follow the promptings of his character."

"No, I'm no individualist, if to be one is to permit men to fall into hurtful habits without offering protest against it. I'm losing faith in that friend Homeyer, who I strongly suspect is a mythical apology for your own short-comings."

"Indeed he's no myth; but a friend who is fond of going into such things and allows me the benefit of his deeper perceptions."

"You having no time, well understood. But if his influence has had the merit of drawing your thoughts from business once in a while we won't quarrel with it."

"Mrs. Lafirme," said Hosmer, seeming moved to pursue the subject, and addressing the spray of white blossoms that adorned Thérèse's black hat, "you admit, I suppose, that in urging your views upon me, you have in mind the advancement of my happiness?"

"Well understood."

"Then why wish to substitute some other form of enjoyment for the one which I find in following my inclinations?"

"Because there is an unsuspected selfishness in your inclinations that works harm to yourself and to those around you. I want you to know," she continued warmly, "the good things of life that cheer and warm, that are always at hand."

"Do you think the happiness of Melicent or—or others could be materially lessened by my fondness for money getting?" he asked dryly, with a faint elevation of eyebrow.

"Yes, in proportion as it deprives them of a charm which any man's society loses, when pursuing one object in life, he grows insensible to every other. But I'll not scold any more. I've made myself troublesome enough for one day. You haven't asked about Melicent. It's true," she laughed, "I haven't given you much chance. She's out on the lake with Grégoire."

"Ah?"

"Yes, in the pirogue. A dangerous little craft, I'm afraid; but she tells me she can swim. I suppose it's all right."

"Oh, Melicent will look after herself."

Hosmer had great faith in his sister Melicent's ability to look after herself; and it must be granted that the young lady fully justified his belief in her.

"She enjoys her visit more than I thought she would," he said.

"Melicent's a dear girl," replied Thérèse cordially, "and a wise one too in guarding herself against a somber influence that I know," with a meaning glance at Hosmer, who was preparing to close his desk.

She suddenly perceived the picture of a handsome boy, far back in one of the pigeon-holes, and with the familiarity born of country intercourse, she looked intently at it, remarking upon the boy's beauty.

"A child whom I loved very much," said Hosmer. "He's dead," and he closed the desk, turning the key in the lock with a sharp click which seemed to add—"and buried."

Thérèse then approached the open door, leaned her back against its casing, and turned her pretty profile towards Hosmer, who, it need not be supposed, was averse to looking at it—only to being caught in the act.

"I want to look in at the mill before work closes," she said; and not waiting for an answer she went on to ask—moved by some association of ideas:—

"How is Joçint doing?"

"Always unruly, the foreman tells me. I don't believe we shall be able to keep him."

Hosmer then spoke a few words through the telephone which connected with the agent's desk at the station, put on his great slouch hat, and thrusting keys and hands into his pocket, joined Thérèse in the door-way.

Quitting the office and making a sharp turn to the left, they came in direct sight of the great mill. She quickly made her way past the huge piles of sawed timber, not waiting for her companion, who loitered at each step of the way, with observant watchfulness. Then mounting the steep stairs that led to the upper portions of the mill, she went at once to her favorite spot, quite on the edge of the open platform that overhung the dam. Here she watched with fascinated delight the great logs hauled dripping from the water, following each till it had changed to the clean symmetry of sawed planks. The unending work made her giddy. For no one was there a moment of rest, and she could well understand the open revolt of the surly Joçint; for he rode the day long on that narrow car, back and forth, back and forth, with his heart in the pine hills and knowing that his little Creole pony was roaming the woods in vicious idleness and his rifle gathering an unsightly rust on the cabin wall at home.

The boy gave but ugly acknowledgment to Thérèse's amiable nod; for he thought she was one upon whom partly rested the fault of this intrusive Industry which had come to fire the souls of indolent fathers with a greedy ambition for gain, at the sore expense of revolting youth.

III

In the Pirogue

Y ou got to set mighty still in this pirogue," said Grégoire, as with a long oar-stroke he pulled out into mid stream.

"Yes, I know," answered Melicent complacently, arranging herself opposite him in the long narrow boat: all sense of danger which the situation might arouse being dulled by the attractiveness of a new experience.

Her resemblance to Hosmer ended with height and slenderness of figure, olive tinted skin, and eyes and hair which were of that dark brown often miscalled black; but unlike his, her face was awake with an eagerness to know and test the novelty and depth of unaccustomed sensation. She had thus far lived an unstable existence, free from the weight of responsibilities, with a notion lying somewhere deep in her consciousness that the world must one day be taken seriously; but that contingency was yet too far away to disturb the harmony of her days.

She had eagerly responded to her brother's suggestion of spending a summer with him in Louisiana. Hitherto, having passed her summers North, West, or East as alternating caprice prompted, she was ready at a word to fit her humor to the novelty of a season at the South. She enjoyed in advance the startling effect which her announced intention produced upon her intimate circle at home; thinking that her whim deserved the distinction of eccentricity with which they chose to invest it. But Melicent was chiefly moved by the prospect of an uninterrupted sojourn with her brother, whom she loved blindly, and to whom she attributed qualities of mind and heart which she thought the world had discovered to use against him.

"You got to set mighty still in this pirogue."

"Yes, I know; you told me so before," and she laughed.

"W'at are you laughin' at?" asked Grégoire with amused but uncertain expectancy.

"Laughing at you, Grégoire; how can I help it?" laughing again.

"Betta wait tell I do somethin' funny, I reckon. Ain't this a putty sight?" he added, referring to the dense canopy of an overarching tree, beneath which they were gliding, and whose extreme branches dipped quite into the slow moving water.

The scene had not attracted Melicent. For she had been engaged in observing her companion rather closely; his personality holding her with a certain imaginative interest.

The young man whom she so closely scrutinized was slightly undersized, but of close and brawny build. His hands were not so refinedly white as those of certain office bred young men of her acquaintance, yet they were not coarsened by undue toil: it being somewhat an axiom with him to do nothing that an available "nigger" might do for him.

Close fitting, high-heeled boots of fine quality incased his feet, in whose shapeliness he felt a pardonable pride; for a young man's excellence was often measured in the circle which he had frequented, by the possession of such a foot. A peculiar grace in the dance and a talent for bold repartee were further characteristics which had made Grégoire's departure keenly felt among certain belles of upper Red River. His features were handsome, of sharp and refined cut; and his eyes black and brilliant as eyes of an alert and intelligent animal sometimes are. Melicent could not reconcile his voice to her liking; it was too softly low and feminine, and carried a note of pleading or pathos, unless he argued with his horse, his dog, or a "nigger," at which times, though not unduly raised, it acquired a biting quality that served the purpose of relieving him from further form of insistence.

He pulled rapidly and in silence down the bayou, that was now so entirely sheltered from the open light of the sky by the meeting branches above, as to seem a dim leafy tunnel fashioned by man's ingenuity. There were no perceptible banks, for the water spread out on either side of them, further than they could follow its flashings through the rank underbrush. The dull plash of some object falling into the water, or the wild call of a lonely bird were the only sounds that broke upon the stillness, beside the monotonous dipping of the oars and the occasional low undertones of their own voices. When Grégoire called the girl's attention to an object near by, she fancied it was the protruding stump of a decaying tree; but reaching for his revolver and taking quiet aim, he drove a ball into the black upturned nozzle that sent it below the surface with an angry splash.

"Will he follow us?" she asked, mildly agitated.

"Oh no; he's glad 'nough to git out o' the way. You betta put down yo' veil," he added a moment later.

Before she could ask a reason—for it was not her fashion to obey at word of command—the air was filled with the doleful hum of a gray swarm of mosquitoes, which attacked them fiercely.

"You didn't tell me the bayou was the refuge of such savage creatures," she said, fastening her veil closely about face and neck, but not before she had felt the sharpness of their angry sting.

"I reckoned you'd 'a knowed all about it: seems like you know everything." After a short interval he added, "you betta take yo' veil off."

She was amused at Grégoire's authoritative tone and she said to him laughing, yet obeying his suggestion, which carried a note of command: "you shall tell me always, why I should do things."

"All right," he replied; "because they ain't any mo' mosquitoes; because I want you to see somethin' worth seein' afta while; and because I like to look at you," which he was doing, with the innocent boldness of a forward child. "Ain't that 'nough reasons?"

"More than enough," she replied shortly.

The rank and clustering vegetation had become denser as they went on, forming an impenetrable tangle on either side, and pressing so closely above that they often needed to lower their heads to avoid the blow of some drooping branch. Then a sudden and unlooked for turn in the bayou carried them out upon the far-spreading waters of the lake, with the broad canopy of the open sky above them.

"Oh," cried Melicent, in surprise. Her exclamation was like a sigh of relief which comes at the removal of some pressure from body or brain.

The wildness of the scene caught upon her erratic fancy, speeding it for a quick moment into the realms of romance. She was an Indian maiden of the far past, fleeing and seeking with her dusky lover some wild and solitary retreat on the borders of this lake, which offered them no seeming foot-hold save such as they would hew themselves with axe or tomahawk. Here and there, a grim cypress lifted its head above the water, and spread wide its moss covered arms inviting refuge to the great black-winged buzzards that circled over and about it in mid-air. Nameless voices—weird sounds that awake in a Southern forest at twilight's approach,—were crying a sinister welcome to the settling gloom.

"This is a place thet can make a man sad, I tell you," said Grégoire, resting his oars, and wiping the moisture from his forehead. "I wouldn't want to be yere alone, not fur any money."

"It is an awful place," replied Melicent with a little appreciative shudder; adding "do you consider me a bodily protection?" and feebly smiling into his face.

"Oh; I ain't 'fraid o' any thing I can see an on'erstan'. I can han'le mos' any thing thet's got a body. But they do tell some mighty queer tales 'bout this lake an' the pine hills yonda."

"Queer—how?"

"W'y, ole McFarlane's buried up there on the hill; an' they's folks 'round yere says he walks about o' nights; can't res' in his grave fur the niggas he's killed."

"Gracious! and who was old McFarlane?"

"The meanest w'ite man thet ever lived, seems like. Used to own this place long befo' the Lafirmes got it. They say he's the person that Mrs. W'at's her name wrote about in Uncle Tom's Cabin."

"Legree? I wonder if it could be true?" Melicent asked with interest.

"Thet's w'at they all say: ask any body."

"You'll take me to his grave, won't you Grégoire," she entreated.

"Well, not this evenin'—I reckon not. It'll have to be broad day, an' the sun shinin' mighty bright w'en I take you to ole McFarlane's grave."

They had retraced their course and again entered the bayou, from which the light had now nearly vanished, making it needful that they watch carefully to escape the hewn logs that floated in numbers upon the water.

"I didn't suppose you were ever sad, Grégoire," Melicent said gently.

"Oh my! yes;" with frank acknowledgment. "You ain't ever seen me w'en I was real lonesome. 'Tain't so bad sence you come. But times w'en I git to thinkin' 'bout home, I'm boun' to cry—seems like I can't he'p it."

"Why did you ever leave home?" she asked sympathetically.

"You see w'en father died, fo' year ago, mother she went back to France, t'her folks there; she never could stan' this country—an' lef' us boys to manage the place. Hec, he took charge the firs' year an' run it in debt. Placide an' me did'n' have no betta luck the naxt year. Then the creditors come up from New Orleans an' took holt. That's the time I packed my duds an' lef'."

"And you came here?"

"No, not at firs'. You see the Santien boys had a putty hard name in the country. Aunt Thérèse, she'd fallen out with father years ago 'bout the way, she said, he was bringin' us up. Father, he wasn't the man to take nothin' from nobody. Never 'lowed any of us to come down yere. I was in Texas, goin' to the devil I reckon, w'en she sent for me, an' yere I am."

"And here you ought to stay, Grégoire."

"Oh, they ain't no betta woman in the worl' then Aunt Thérèse, w'en you do like she wants. See 'em yonda waitin' fur us? Reckon they thought we was drowned."

IV

A Small Interruption

When Melicent came to visit her brother, Mrs. Lafirme persuaded him to abandon his uncomfortable quarters at the mill and take up his residence in the cottage, which stood just beyond the lawn of the big house. This cottage had been furnished *de pied en cap* many years before, in readiness against an excess of visitors, which in days gone by was not of infrequent occurrence at Place-du-Bois. It was Melicent's delighted intention to keep house here. And she foresaw no obstacle in the way of procuring the needed domestic aid in a place which was clearly swarming with idle women and children.

"Got a cook yet, Mel?" was Hosmer's daily enquiry on returning home, to which Melicent was as often forced to admit that she had no cook, but was not without abundant hope of procuring one.

Betsy's Aunt Cynthy had promised with a sincerity which admitted not of doubt, that "de Lord willin'" she would "be on han' Monday, time to make de mornin' coffee." Which assurance had afforded Melicent a Sunday free of disturbing doubts concerning the future of her undertaking. But who may know what the morrow will bring forth? Cynthy had been "tuck sick in de night." So ran the statement of the wee pickaninny who appeared at Melicent's gate many hours later than morning coffee time: delivering his message in a high voice of complaint, and disappearing like a vision without further word.

Uncle Hiram, then called to the breach, had staked his patriarchal honor on the appearance of his niece Suze on Tuesday. Melicent and Thérèse meeting Suze some days later in a field path, asked the cause of her bad faith. The girl showed them all the white teeth which nature had lavished on her, saying with the best natured laugh in the world: "I don' know how come I didn' git dere Chewsday like I promise."

If the ladies were not disposed to consider that an all-sufficient reason, so much the worse, for Suze had no other to offer.

From Mose's wife, Minervy, better things might have been expected. But after a solemn engagement to take charge of Melicent's kitchen on Wednesday, the dusky matron suddenly awoke to the need of "holpin' Mose hoe out dat co'n in de stiff lan'."

Thérèse, seeing that the girl was really eager to play in the brief role of housekeeper had used her powers, persuasive and authoritative, to procure servants for her, but without avail. She herself was not without an abundance of them, from the white-haired Hiram, whose position on the place had long been a sinecure, down to the little brown legged tot Mandy, much given to falling asleep in the sun, when not chasing venturesome poultry off forbidden ground, or stirring gentle breezes with an enormous palm leaf fan about her mistress during that lady's after dinner nap.

When pressed to give a reason for this apparent disinclination of the negroes to work for the Hosmers, Nathan, who was at the moment being interviewed on the front veranda by Thérèse and Melicent, spoke out.

"Dey 'low 'roun' yere, dat you's mean to de black folks, ma'am: dat what dey says—I don' know me."

"Mean," cried Melicent, amazed, "in what way, pray?"

"Oh, all sort o' ways," he admitted, with a certain shy brazenness; determined to go through with the ordeal.

"Dey 'low you wants to cut de little gals' plaits off, an' sich—I don' know me."

"Do you suppose, Nathan," said Thérèse attempting but poorly to hide her amusement at Melicent's look of dismay, "that Miss Hosmer would bother herself with darkies' plaits?"

"Dat's w'at I tink m'sef. Anyways, I'll sen' Ar'minty 'roun' to-morrow, sho."

Melicent was not without the guilty remembrance of having one day playfully seized one of the small Mandy's bristling plaits, daintily between finger and thumb, threatening to cut them all away with the scissors which she carried. Yet she could not but believe that there was some deeper motive underlying this systematic reluctance of the negroes to give their work in exchange for the very good pay which she offered. Thérèse soon enlightened her with the information that the negroes were very averse to working for Northern people whose speech, manners, and attitude towards themselves were unfamiliar. She was given the consoling assurance of not being the only victim of this boycott, as Thérèse recalled many examples of strangers whom she knew to have met with a like cavalier treatment at the darkies' hands.

Needless to say, Araminty never appeared.

V

IN THE PINE WOODS

When Grégoire said to Melicent that there was no better woman in the world than his Aunt Thérèse, "W'en you do like she wants," the statement was so incomplete as to leave one in uncomfortable doubt of the expediency of venturing within the influence of so exacting a nature. True, Thérèse required certain conduct from others, but she was willing to further its accomplishment by personal efforts, even sacrifices—that could leave no doubt of the pure unselfishness of her motive. There was hardly a soul at Place-du-Bois who had not felt the force of her will and yielded to its gentle influence.

The picture of Joçint as she had last seen him, stayed with her, till it gave form to a troubled desire moving her to see him again and speak with him. He had always been an unruly subject, inclined to a surreptitious defiance of authority. Repeatedly had he been given work on the plantation and as many times dismissed for various causes. Thérèse would have long since removed him had it not been for his old father Morico, whose long life spent on the place had established a claim upon her tolerance.

In the late afternoon, when the shadows of the magnolias were stretching in grotesque lengths across the lawn, Thérèse stood waiting for Uncle Hiram to bring her sleek bay Beauregard around to the front. The dark close fitting habit which she wore lent brilliancy to her soft blonde coloring; and there was no mark of years about her face or figure, save the settling of a thoughtful shadow upon the eyes, which joys and sorrows that were past and gone had left there.

As she rode by the cottage, Melicent came out on the porch to wave a laughing good-bye. The girl was engaged in effacing the simplicity of her rooms with certain bizarre decorations that seemed the promptings of a disordered imagination. Yards of fantastic calico had been brought up from the store, which Grégoire with hammer and tacks was amiably forming into impossible designs at the prompting of the girl. The little darkies had been enlisted to bring their contributions of palm branches, pine cones, ferns, and bright hued bird wings—and a row of those small recruits stood on the porch, gaping in wide-mouthed admiration at a sight that stirred within their breasts such remnant of savage instinct as past generations had left there in dormant survival.

One of the small audience permitted her attention to be drawn for a moment from the gorgeous in-door spectacle, to follow the movements of her mistress.

"Jis' look Miss T'rèse how she go a lopin' down de lane. Dere she go—dere she go—now she gone," and she again became contemplative.

Thérèse, after crossing the railroad, for a space kept to the brow of the hill where stretched a well defined road, which by almost imperceptible degrees led deeper and always higher into the woods. Presently, leaving this road and turning into a bridle path where an unpracticed eye would have discovered no sign of travel, she rode on until reaching a small clearing among the pines, in the center of which stood a very old and weather beaten cabin.

Here she dismounted, before Morico knew of her presence, for he sat with his back partly turned to the open door. As she entered and greeted him, he arose from his chair, all trembling with excitement at her visit; the long white locks, straggling and unkept, falling about his brown visage that had grown old and weather beaten with his cabin. Sinking down into his seat—the hide covered chair that had been worn smooth by years of usefulness—he gazed well pleased at Thérèse, who seated herself beside him.

"Ah, this is quite the handsomest you have made yet, Morico," she said addressing him in French, and taking up the fan that he was curiously fashioning of turkey feathers.

"I am taking extra pains with it," he answered, looking complacently at his handiwork and smoothing down the glossy feathers with the ends of his withered old fingers. "I thought the American lady down at the house might want to buy it."

Thérèse could safely assure him of Melicent's willingness to seize on the trophy.

Then she asked why Joçint had not been to the house with news of him. "I have had chickens and eggs for you, and no way of sending them."

At mention of his son's name, the old man's face clouded with displeasure and his hand trembled so that he was at some pains to place the feather which he was at the moment adding to the widening fan.

"Joçint is a bad son, madame, when even you have been able to do nothing with him. The trouble that boy has given me no one knows; but let him not think I am too old to give him a sound drubbing."

Joçint meanwhile had returned from the mill and seeing Thérèse's horse fastened before his door, was at first inclined to skulk back into the woods; but an impulse of defiance moved him to enter, and gave to his ugly countenance a look that was far from agreeable as he mumbled a greeting to Thérèse. His father he did not address. The old man looked from son to visitor with feeble expectancy of some good to come from her presence there.

Joçint's straight and coarse black hair hung in a heavy mop over his low retreating forehead, almost meeting the ill-defined line of eyebrow that straggled above small dusky black eyes, that with the rest of his physique was an inheritance from his Indian mother.

Approaching the safe or *garde manger*, which was the most prominent piece of furniture in the room, he cut a wedge from the round loaf of heavy soggy corn bread that he found there, added a layer of fat pork, and proceeded to devour the unpalatable morsel with hungry relish.

"That is but poor fare for your old father, Joçint," said Thérèse, looking steadily at the youth.

"Well, I got no chance me, fu' go fine nuttin in de 'ood" (woods), he answered purposely in English, to annoy his father who did not understand the language.

"But you are earning enough to buy him something better; and you know there is always plenty at the house that I am willing to spare him."

"I got no chance me fu' go to de 'ouse neider," he replied deliberately, after washing down the scant repast with a long draught from the tin bucket which he had replenished at the cistern before entering. He swallowed the water regardless of the "wiggles" whose presence was plainly visible.

"What does he say?" asked Morico scanning Thérèse's face appealingly.

"He only says that work at the mill keeps him a good deal occupied," she said with attempted carelessness.

As she finished speaking, Joçint put on his battered felt hat, and strode out the back door; his gun on his shoulder and a yellow cur following close at his heels.

Thérèse remained a while longer with the old man, hearing sympathetically the long drawn story of his troubles, and cheering him as no one else in the world was able to do, then she went away.

Joçint was not the only one who had seen Beauregard fastened at Morico's door. Hosmer was making a tour of inspection that afternoon through the woods, and when he came suddenly upon Thérèse some moments after she had quitted the cabin, the meeting was not so wholly accidental as that lady fancied it was.

If there could be a situation in which Hosmer felt more than in another at ease in Thérèse's company, it was the one in which he found himself. There was no need to seek occupation for his hands, those members being sufficiently engaged with the management of his horse. His eyes found legitimate direction in following the various details which a rider is presumed to observe; and his manner freed from the necessity of self direction took upon itself an ease which was occasional enough to mark it as noteworthy.

She told him of her visit. At mention of Joçint's name he reddened: then followed the acknowledgment that the youth in question had caused him to lose his temper and forget his dignity during the afternoon.

"In what way?" asked Thérèse. "It would be better to dismiss him than to rail at him. He takes reproof badly and is extremely treacherous."

"Mill hands are not plentiful, or I should send him off at once. Oh, he is an unbearable fellow. The men told me of a habit he has of letting the logs roll off the carriage, causing a good deal of annoyance and delay in replacing them. I was willing enough to believe it might be accidental, until I caught him today in the very act. I am thankful not to have knocked him down."

Hosmer felt exhilarated. The excitement of his encounter with Joçint had not yet died away; this softly delicious atmosphere; the subtle aroma of the pines; his unlooked for meeting with Thérèse—all combined to stir him with unusual emotions.

"What a splendid creature Beauregard is," he said, smoothing the animal's glossy mane with the end of his riding whip. The horses were walking slowly in step, and close together.

"Of course he is," said Thérèse proudly, patting the arched neck of her favorite. "Beauregard is a blooded animal, remember. He quite throws poor Nelson in the shade," looking pityingly at Hosmer's heavily built iron-grey.

"Don't cast any slurs on Nelson, Mrs. Lafirme. He's done me service that's worthy of praise—worthy of better treatment than he gets."

"I know. He deserves the best, poor fellow. When you go away you should turn him out to pasture, and forbid any one to use him."

"It would be a good idea; but—I'm not so certain about going away."

"Oh I beg your pardon. I fancied your movements were directed by some unchangeable laws."

"Like the planets in their orbits? No, there is no absolute need of my going; the business which would have called me away can be done as readily by letter. If I heed my inclination it certainly holds me here."

"I don't understand that. It's natural enough that I should be fond of the country; but you—I don't believe you've been away for three months, have you? and city life certainly has its attractions."

"It's beastly," he answered decidedly. "I greatly prefer the country—this country; though I can imagine a condition under which it would be less agreeable; insupportable, in fact."

He was looking fixedly at Thérèse, who let her eyes rest for an instant in the unaccustomed light of his, while she asked "and the condition?"

"If you were to go away. Oh! it would take the soul out of my life."

It was now her turn to look in all directions save the one in which his glance invited her. At a slight and imperceptible motion of the bridle, well understood by Beauregard, the horse sprang forward into a quick canter, leaving Nelson and his rider to follow as they could.

Hosmer overtook her when she stopped to let her horse drink at the side of the hill where the sparkling spring water came trickling from the moist rocks, and emptied into the long out-scooped trunk of a cypress, that served as trough. The two horses plunged their heads deep in the clear water; the proud Beauregard quivering with satisfaction, as arching his neck and shaking off the clinging moisture, he waited for his more deliberate companion.

"Doesn't it give one a sympathetic pleasure," said Thérèse, "to see the relish with which they drink?"

"I never thought of it," replied Hosmer, cynically. His face was unusually flushed, and diffidence was plainly seizing him again.

Thérèse was now completely mistress of herself, and during the remainder of the ride she talked incessantly, giving him no chance for more than the briefest answers.

VI

Melicent Talks

"David Hosmer, you are the most supremely unsatisfactory man existing."

Hosmer had come in from his ride, and seating himself in the large wicker chair that stood in the center of the room, became at once absorbed in reflections. Being addressed, he looked up at his sister, who sat sidewards on the edge of a table slightly removed, swaying a dainty slippered foot to and fro in evident impatience.

"What crime have I committed now, Melicent, against your code?" he asked, not fully aroused from his reverie.

"You've committed nothing; your sin is one of omission. I absolutely believe you go through the world with your eyes, to all practical purposes, closed. Don't you notice anything; any change?"

"To be sure I do," said Hosmer, relying on a knowledge lent him by previous similar experiences, and taking in the clinging artistic drapery that enfolded her tall spare figure, "you've a new gown on. I didn't think to mention it, but I noticed it all the same."

This admission of a discernment that he had failed to make evident, aroused Melicent's uncontrolled mirth.

"A new gown!" and she laughed heartily. "A threadbare remnant! A thing that holds by shreds and tatters."

She went behind her brother's chair, taking his face between her hands, and turning it upward, kissed him on the forehead. With his head in such position, he could not fail to observe the brilliant folds of muslin that were arranged across the ceiling to simulate the canopy of a tent. Still holding his face, she moved it sidewards, so that his eyes, knowing now what office was expected of them, followed the line of decorations about the room.

"It's immense, Mel; perfectly immense. When did you do it all?"

"This afternoon, with Grégoire's help," she answered, looking proudly at her work. "And my poor hands are in such condition! But really, Dave," she continued, seating herself on the side of his chair, with an arm about his neck, and he leaning his head back on the improvised cushion, "I wonder that you ever got on in business, observing things as little as you do."

"Oh, that's different."

"Well, I don't believe you see half that you ought to," adding naively, "How did you and Mrs. Lafirme happen to come home together this evening?"

The bright lamp-light made the flush quite evident that arose to his face under her near gaze.

"We met in the woods; she was coming from Morico's."

"David, do you know that woman is an angel. She's simply the most perfect creature I ever knew."

Melicent's emphasis of speech was a thing so recurrent, so singularly her own, as to startle an unaccustomed hearer.

"That opinion might carry some weight, Mel, if I hadn't heard it scores of times from you, and of as many different women."

"Indeed you have not. Mrs. Lafirme is exceptional. Really, when she stands at the end of the veranda, giving orders to those darkies, her face a little flushed, she's positively a queen."

"As far as queenliness may be compatible with the angelic state," replied Hosmer, but not ill pleased with Melicent's exaggerated praise of Thérèse.

Neither had heard a noiseless step approaching, and they only became aware of an added human presence, when Mandy's small voice was heard to issue from Mandy's small body which stood in the mingled light and shadow of the door-way.

"Aunt B'lindy 'low supper on de table gittin' cole."

"Come here, Mandy," cried Melicent, springing after the child. But Mandy was flying back through the darkness. She was afraid of Melicent.

Laughing heartily, the girl disappeared into her bedroom, to make some needed additions to her toilet; and Hosmer, waiting for her, returned to his interrupted reflections. The words which he had spoken during a moment of emotion to Thérèse, out in the piny woods, had served a double purpose with him. They had shown him more plainly than he had quite been certain of, the depth of his feeling for her; and also had they settled his determination. He was not versed in the reading of a woman's nature, and he found himself at a loss to interpret Thérèse's actions. He recalled how she had looked away from him when he had spoken the few tender words that were yet whirling in his memory; how she had impetuously ridden ahead,—leaving him to follow alone; and her incessant speech that had forced him into silence. All of which might or might not be symptoms in his favor. He remembered her kind solicitude for his comfort and happiness during the past year; but he as readily recalled that he had not been the only recipient of such favors. His reflections led to no certainty, except that he loved her and meant to tell her so.

Thérèse's door being closed, and moreover locked, Aunt Belindy, the stout negress who had superintended the laying of supper, felt free to give low speech to her wrath as she went back and forth between dining-room and kitchen.

"Suppa gittin' dat cole 'tain' gwine be fittin' fu' de dogs te' tech. Believe half de time w'ite folks ain't got no feelin's, no how. If dey speck I'se gwine stan' up heah on my two feet all night, dey's foolin' dey sef. I ain't gwine do it. Git out dat doo' you Mandy! you want me dash dis heah coffee pot at you—blockin' up de doo's dat away? W'ar dat good fu' nuttin Betsy? Look yonda, how she done flung dem dere knife an forks on de table. Jis let Miss T'rèse kotch'er. Good God A'mighty, Miss T'rèse mus' done gone asleep. G'long dar an' see."

There was no one on the plantation who would have felt at liberty to enter Thérèse's bedroom without permission, the door being closed; yet she had taken the needless precaution of bringing lock and bolt to the double security of her moment of solitude. The first announcement of supper had found her still in her riding habit, with head thrown back upon the cushion of her lounging chair, and her mind steeped in a semi-stupor that it would be injustice to her brighter moments to call reflection.

Thérèse was a warm-hearted woman, and a woman of clear mental vision; a combination not found so often together as to make it ordinary. Being a woman of warm heart, she had loved her husband with the devotion which good husbands deserve; but being a clear-headed woman, she was not disposed to rebel against the changes which Time brings, when so disposed, to the human sensibilities. She was not steeped in that agony of remorse which many might consider becoming in a widow of five years' standing at the discovery that her heart which had fitted well the holding of a treasure, was not narrowed to the holding of a memory,—the treasure being gone.

Mandy's feeble knock at the door was answered by her mistress in person who had now banished all traces of her ride and its resultant cogitations.

The two women, with Hosmer and Grégoire, sat out on the veranda after supper as their custom was during these warm summer evenings.

There was no attempt at sustained conversation; they talked by snatches to and at one another, of the day's small events; Melicent and Grégoire having by far the most to say. The girl was half reclining in the hammock which she kept in a slow, unceasing motion by the impetus of her slender foot; he sitting some distance removed on the steps. Hosmer was noticeably silent; even Joçint as a theme failing to rouse him to more than a few words of dismissal. His will and tenacity were controlling him to one bent. He had made up his mind that he had something to say to Mrs. Lafirme, and he was impatient at any enforced delay in the telling.

Grégoire slept now in the office of the mill, as a measure of precaution. To-night, Hosmer had received certain late telegrams that necessitated a return to the mill, and his iron-grey was standing outside in the lane with Grégoire's horse, awaiting the pleasure of his rider. When Grégoire quitted the group to go and throw the saddles across the patient animals, Melicent, who contemplated an additional hour's chat with Thérèse, crossed over to the cottage to procure a light wrap for her sensitive shoulders against the chill night air. Hosmer, who had started to the assistance of Grégoire, seeing that Thérèse had remained alone, standing at the top of the stairs, approached her. Remaining a few steps below her, and looking up into her face, he held out his hand to say good-night, which was an unusual proceeding, for they had not shaken hands since his return to Place-du-Bois three months before. She gave him her soft hand to hold and as the warm, moist palm met his, it acted like a charged electric battery turning its subtle force upon his sensitive nerves.

"Will you let me talk to you to-morrow?" he asked.

"Yes, perhaps; if I have time."

"Oh, you will make the time. I can't let the day go by without telling you many things that you ought to have known long ago." The battery was still doing its work. "And I can't let the night go by without telling you that I love you."

Grégoire called out that the horses were ready. Melicent was approaching in her diaphanous envelope, and Hosmer reluctantly let drop Thérèse's hand and left her.

As the men rode away, the two women stood silently following their diminishing outlines into the darkness and listening to the creaking of the saddles and the dull regular thud of the horses' feet upon the soft earth, until the sounds grew inaudible, when they turned to the inner shelter of the veranda. Melicent once more possessed herself of the hammock in which she now reclined fully, and Thérèse sat near enough beside her to intertwine her fingers between the tense cords.

"What a great difference in age there must be between you and your brother," she said, breaking the silence.

"Yes—though he is younger and I older than you perhaps think. He was fifteen and the only child when I was born. I am twenty-four, so he of course is thirty-nine."

"I certainly thought him older."

"Just imagine, Mrs. Lafirme, I was only ten when both my parents died. We had no kindred living in the West, and I positively rebelled against being separated from David; so you see he's had the care of me for a good many years."

"He appears very fond of you."

"Oh, not only that, but you've no idea how splendidly he's done for me in every way. Looked after my interest and all that, so that I'm perfectly independent. Poor Dave," she continued, heaving a profound sigh, "he's had more than his share of trouble, if ever a man had. I wonder when his day of compensation will come."

"Don't you think," ventured Thérèse, "that we make too much of our individual trials. We are all so prone to believe our own burden heavier than our neighbor's."

"Perhaps—but there can be no question about the weight of David's. I'm not a bit selfish about him though; poor fellow, I only wish he'd marry again."

Melicent's last words stung Thérèse like an insult. Her native pride rebelled against the reticence of this man who had shared her confidence while keeping her in ignorance of so important a feature of his own life. But her dignity would not permit a show of disturbance; she only asked:—

"How long has his wife been dead?"

"Oh," cried Melicent, in dismay. "I thought you knew of course; why—she isn't dead at all—they were divorced two years ago."

The girl felt intuitively that she had yielded to an indiscretion of speech. She could not know David's will in the matter, but since he had all along left Mrs. Lafirme in ignorance of his domestic trials, she concluded it was not for her to enlighten that lady further. Her next remark was to call Thérèse's attention to the unusual number of glow-worms that were flashing through the darkness, and to ask the sign of it, adding "every thing seems to be the sign of something down here."

"Aunt Belindy might tell you," replied Thérèse, "I only know that I feel the signs of being very sleepy after that ride through the woods to-day. Don't mind if I say good night?"

"Certainly not. Good night, dear Mrs. Lafirme. Let me stay here till David comes back; I should die of fright, to go to the cottage alone."

VII

Painful Disclosures

Thérèse possessed an independence of thought exceptional enough when considered in relation to her life and its surrounding conditions. But as a woman who lived in close contact with her fellow-beings she was little given to the consideration of abstract ideas, except in so far as they touched the individual man. If ever asked to give her opinion of divorce, she might have replied that the question being one which did not immediately concern her, its remoteness had removed it from the range of her inquiry. She felt vaguely that in many cases it might be a blessing; conceding that it must not infrequently be a necessity, to be appealed to however only in an extremity beyond which endurance could scarcely hold. With the prejudices of her Catholic education coloring her sentiment, she instinctively shrank when the theme confronted her as one having even a remote reference to her own clean existence. There was no question with her of dwelling upon the matter; it was simply a thing to be summarily dismissed and as far as possible effaced from her remembrance.

Thérèse had not reached the age of thirty-five without learning that life presents many insurmountable obstacles which must be accepted, whether with the callousness of philosophy, the revolt of weakness or the dignity of self-respect. The following morning, the only sign which she gave of her mental disturbance, was an appearance that might have succeeded a night of unrefreshing sleep.

Hosmer had decided that his interview with Mrs. Lafirme should not be left further to the caprice of accident. An hour or more before noon he rode up from the mill knowing it to be a time when he would likely find her alone. Not seeing her he proceeded to make inquiry of the servants; first appealing to Betsy.

"I don' know whar Miss T'rèse," with a rising inflection on the "whar." "I yain't seed her sence mornin', time she sont Unc' Hi'um yonda to old Morico wid de light bread an' truck," replied the verbose Betsy. "Aunt B'lindy, you know whar Miss T'rèse?"

"How you want me know? standin' up everlastin' in de kitchen a bakin' light-bread fu' lazy trash det betta be in de fiel' wurkin' a crap like people, stid o' 'pendin' on yeda folks."

Mandy, who had been a silent listener, divining that she had perhaps better make known certain information that was exclusively her own piped out:—

"Miss T'rèse shet up in de parla; 'low she want we all lef 'er 'lone."

Having as it were forced an entrance into the stronghold where Thérèse had supposed herself secure from intrusion, Hosmer at once seated himself beside her.

This was a room kept for the most part closed during the summer days when the family lived chiefly on the verandas or in the wide open hall There lingered about it the foreign scent of cool clean matting, mingled with a faint odor of rose which came from a curious Japanese jar that stood on the ample hearth. Through the green half-closed shutters the air came in gentle ripples, sweeping the filmy curtains back and forth in irregular undulations. A few tasteful pictures hung upon the walls, alternating with family portraits, for the most part stiff and unhandsome, except in the case of such as were of so remote date that age gave them a claim upon the interest and admiration of a far removed generation.

It was not entirely clear to the darkies whether this room were not a sort of holy sanctuary, where one should scarce be permitted to breathe, except under compulsion of a driving necessity.

"Mrs. Lafirme," began Hosmer, "Melicent tells me that she made you acquainted last night with the matter which I wished to talk to you about to-day."

"Yes," Thérèse replied, closing the book which she had made a pretense of reading, and laying it down upon the window-sill near which she sat; adding very simply, "Why did you not tell me long ago, Mr. Hosmer?"

"God knows," he replied; the sharp conviction breaking upon him, that this disclosure had some how changed the aspect of life for him. "Natural reluctance to speak of a thing so painful—native reticence—I don't know what. I hope you forgive me; that you will let it make no difference in whatever regard you may have for me."

"I had better tell you at once that there must be no repetition of—of what you told me last night."

Hosmer had feared it. He made no protest in words; his revolt was inward and showed itself only in an added pallor and increased rigidity of face lines. He arose and went to a near window, peering for a while aimlessly out between the partly open slats.

"I hadn't thought of your being a Catholic," he said, finally turning towards her with folded arms.

"Because you have never seen any outward signs of it. But I can't leave you under a false impression: religion doesn't influence my reason in this."

"Do you think then that a man who has had such misfortune, should be debarred the happiness which a second marriage could give him?"

"No, nor a woman either, if it suit her moral principle, which I hold to be something peculiarly one's own."

"That seems to me to be a prejudice," he replied. "Prejudices may be set aside by an effort of the will," catching at a glimmer of hope.

"There are some prejudices which a woman can't afford to part with, Mr. Hosmer," she said a little haughtily, "even at the price of happiness. Please say no more about it, think no more of it."

He seated himself again, facing her; and looking at him all her sympathetic nature was moved at sight of his evident trouble.

"Tell me about it. I would like to know every thing in your life," she said, feelingly.

"It's very good of you," he said, holding a hand for a moment over his closed eyes. Then looking up abruptly, "It was a painful enough experience, but I never dreamed that it could have had this last blow in reserve for me."

"When did you marry?" she asked, wishing to start him with the story which she fancied he would feel better for the telling.

"Ten years ago. I am a poor hand to analyze character: my own or another's. My reasons for doing certain things have never been quite clear to me; or I have never schooled myself to inquiry into my own motives for action. I have been always thoroughly the business man. I don't make a boast of it, but I have no reason to be ashamed of the admission. Socially, I have mingled little with my fellow-beings, especially with women, whose society has had little attraction for me; perhaps, because I have never been thrown much into it, and I was nearly thirty when I first met my wife."

"Was it in St. Louis?" Thérèse asked.

"Yes. I had been inveigled into going on a river excursion," he said, plunging into the story, "Heaven knows how. Perhaps I was feeling unwell—I really can't remember. But at all events I met a friend who introduced me early in the day to a young girl—Fanny Larimore. She was a pretty little thing, not more than twenty, all pink and white and merry blue eyes and stylish clothes. Whatever it was, there was something about her that kept me at her side all day. Every word and movement of hers had an exaggerated importance for me. I fancied such things had never been said or done quite in the same way before."

"You were in love," sighed Thérèse. Why the sigh she could not have told.

"I presume so. Well, after that, I found myself thinking of her at the most inopportune moments. I went to see her again and again—my first impression deepened, and in two weeks I had asked her to marry me. I can safely say, we knew nothing of each other's character. After marriage, matters went well enough for a while." Hosmer here arose, and walked the length of the room.

"Mrs. Lafirme," he said, "can't you understand that it must be a painful thing for a man to disparage one woman to another: the woman who has been his wife to the woman he loves? Spare me the rest."

"Please have no reservations with me; I shall not misjudge you in any case," an inexplicable something was moving her to know what remained to be told.

"It wasn't long before she attempted to draw me into what she called society," Hosmer continued. "I am little versed in defining shades of distinction between classes, but I had seen from the beginning that Fanny's associates were not of the best social rank by any means. I had vaguely expected her to turn from them, I suppose, when she married. Naturally, I resisted anything so distasteful as being dragged through rounds of amusement that had no sort of attraction whatever for me. Besides, my business connections were extending, and they claimed the greater part of my time and thoughts.

"A year after our marriage our boy was born." Here Hosmer ceased speaking for a while, seemingly under pressure of a crowding of painful memories.

"The child whose picture you have at the office?" asked Thérèse.

"Yes," and he resumed with plain effort: "It seemed for a while that the baby would give its mother what distraction she sought so persistently away from home; but its influence did not last and she soon grew as restless as before. Finally there was nothing that united us except the child. I can't really say that we were united through him, but our love for the boy was the one feeling that we had in common. When he was three years old, he died. Melicent had come to live with us after leaving school. She was a high-spirited girl full of conceits as she is now, and in her exaggerated way became filled with horror of what she called the mésalliance I had made. After a month she went away to live with friends. I didn't oppose her. I saw little of my wife, being often away from home; but as feebly observant as I was, I had now and again marked a peculiarity of manner about her that vaguely troubled me. She seemed to avoid me and we grew more and more divided.

"One day I returned home rather early. Melicent was with me. We found Fanny in the dining-room lying on the sofa. As we entered, she looked at us wildly and in striving to get up grasped aimlessly at the back of a chair. I felt on a sudden as if there were some awful calamity threatening my existence. I suppose, I looked helplessly at Melicent, managing to ask her what was the matter with my wife. Melicent's black eyes were flashing indignation. 'Can't you see she's been drinking. God help you,' she said. Mrs. Lafirme, you know now the reason which drove me away from home and kept me away. I never permitted my wife to want for the comforts of life during my absence; but she sued for divorce some years ago and it was granted, with alimony which I doubled. You know the miserable story now. Pardon me for dragging it to such a length. I don't see why I should have told it after all."

Thérèse had remained perfectly silent; rigid at times, listening to Hosmer often with closed eyes.

He waited for her to speak, but she said nothing for a while till finally: "Your—your wife is still quite young—do her parents live with her?"

"Oh no, she has none. I suppose she lives alone."

"And those habits; you don't know if she continues them?"

"I dare say she does. I know nothing of her, except that she receipts for the amount paid her each month."

The look of painful thought deepened on Thérèse's face but her questions having been answered, she again became silent.

Hosmer's eyes were imploring her for a look, but she would not answer them.

"Haven't you a word to say to me?" he entreated.

"No, I have nothing to say, except what would give you pain."

"I can bear anything from you," he replied, at a loss to guess her meaning.

"The kindest thing I can say, Mr. Hosmer, is, that I hope you have acted blindly. I hate to believe that the man I care for, would deliberately act the part of a cruel egotist."

"I don't understand you."

"I have learned one thing through your story, which appears very plain to me," she replied. "You married a woman of weak character. You furnished her with every means to increase that weakness, and shut her out absolutely from your life and yourself from hers. You left her then as practically without moral support as you have certainly done now, in deserting her. It was the act of a coward." Thérèse spoke the last words with intensity.

"Do you think that a man owes nothing to himself?" Hosmer asked, in resistance to her accusation.

"Yes. A man owes to his manhood, to face the consequences of his own actions."

Hosmer had remained seated. He did not even with glance follow Thérèse who had arisen and was moving restlessly about the room. He had so long seen himself as a martyr; his mind had become so habituated to the picture, that he could not of a sudden look at a different one, believing that it could be the true one. Nor was he eager to accept a view of the situation that would place him in his own eyes in a contemptible light. He tried to think that Thérèse must be wrong; but even admitting a doubt of her being right, her words carried an element of truth that he was not able to shut out from his conscience. He felt her to be a woman with moral perceptions keener than his own and his love, which in the past twenty-four hours had grown to overwhelm him, moved him now to a blind submission.

"What would you have me do, Mrs. Lafirme?"

"I would have you do what is right," she said eagerly, approaching him.

"O, don't present me any questions of right and wrong; can't you see that I'm blind?" he said, self accusingly. "What ever I do, must be because you want it; because I love you."

She was standing beside him and he took her hand.

"To do a thing out of love for you, would be the only comfort and strength left me."

"Don't say that," she entreated. "Love isn't everything in life; there is something higher."

"God in heaven, there shouldn't be!" he exclaimed, passionately pressing her hand to his forehead, his cheek, his lips.

"Oh, don't make it harder for me," Thérèse said softly, attempting to withdraw her hand.

It was her first sign of weakness, and he seized on it for his advantage. He arose quickly—unhesitatingly—and took her in his arms.

For a moment that was very brief, there was danger that the task of renunciation would not only be made harder, but impossible, for both; for it was in utter blindness to everything but love for each other, that their lips met.

The great plantation bell was clanging out the hour of noon; the hour for sweet and restful enjoyment; but to Hosmer, the sound was like the voice of a derisive demon, mocking his anguish of spirit, as he mounted his horse, and rode back to the mill.

VIII

Treats of Melicent

Melicent knew that there were exchanges of confidence going on between her brother and Mrs. Lafirme, from which she was excluded. She had noted certain lengthy conferences held in remote corners of the verandas. The two had deliberately withdrawn one moonlight evening to pace to and fro the length of gravel walk that stretched from door front to lane; and Melicent had fancied that they rather lingered when under the deep shadow of the two great live-oaks that overarched the gate. But that of course was fancy; a young girl's weakness to think the world must go as she would want it to.

She was quite sure of having heard Mrs. Lafirme say "I will help you." Could it be that David had fallen into financial straights and wanted assistance from Thérèse? No, that was improbable and furthermore, distasteful, so Melicent would not burden herself with the suspicion. It was far more agreeable to believe that affairs were shaping themselves according to her wishes regarding her brother and her friend. Yet her mystification was in no wise made clearer, when David left them to go to St. Louis.

Melicent was not ready or willing to leave with him. She had not had her "visit out" as she informed him, when he proposed it to her. To remain in the cottage during his absence was out of the question, so she removed herself and all her pretty belongings over to the house, taking possession of one of the many spare rooms. The act of removal furnished her much entertainment of a mild sort, into which, however, she successfully infused something of her own intensity by making the occasion one to bring a large detachment of the plantation force into her capricious service.

Melicent was going out, and she stood before her mirror to make sure that she looked properly. She was black from head to foot. From the great ostrich plume that nodded over her wide-brimmed hat, to the pointed toe of the patent leather boot that peeped from under her gown—a filmy gauzy thing setting loosely to her slender shapely figure. She laughed at the somberness of her reflection, which she at once set about relieving with a great bunch of geraniums—big and scarlet and long-stemmed, that she thrust slantwise through her belt.

Melicent, always charming, was very pretty when she laughed. She thought so herself and laughed a second time into the depths of her dark handsome eyes. One corner of the large mouth turned saucily upward, and the lips holding their own crimson and all that the cheeks were lacking, parted only a little over the gleaming whiteness of her teeth. As she looked at herself critically, she thought that a few more pounds of flesh would have well become her. It had been only the other day that her slimness was altogether to her liking; but at present she was in love with plumpness as typified in Mrs. Lafirme. However, on the whole, she was not ill pleased with her appearance, and gathering up her gloves and parasol, she quitted the room.

It was "broad day," one of the requirements which Grégoire had named as essential for taking Melicent to visit old McFarlane's grave. But the sun was not "shining mighty bright," the second condition, and whose absence they were willing enough to overlook, seeing that the month was September.

They had climbed quite to the top of the hill, and stood on the very brink of the deep toilsome railroad cut all fringed with matted grass and young pines, that had but lately sprung there. Up and down the track, as far as they could see on either side the steel rails glittered on into gradual dimness. There were patches of the field before them, white with bursting cotton which scores of negroes, men, women and children were dexterously picking and thrusting into great bags that hung from their shoulders and dragged beside them on the ground; no machine having yet been found to surpass the sufficiency of five human fingers for wrenching the cotton from its tenacious hold. Elsewhere, there were squads "pulling fodder" from the dry corn stalks; hot and distasteful work enough. In the nearest field, where the cotton was young and green, with no show of ripening, the overseer rode slowly between the rows, sprinkling plentifully the dry powder of paris green from two muslin bags attached to the ends of a short pole that lay before him across the saddle.

Grégoire's presence would be needed later in the day, when the cotton was hauled to gin to be weighed; when the mules were brought to stable, to see them properly fed and cared for, and the gearing all put in place. In the meanwhile he was deliciously idle with Melicent.

They retreated into the woods, soon losing sight of everything but the trees that surrounded them and the underbrush, that was scant and scattered over the turf which the height of the trees permitted to grow green and luxuriant.

There, on the far slope of the hill they found McFarlane's grave, which they knew to be such only by the battered and weather-worn cross of wood, that lurched disreputably to one side—there being no hand in all the world that cared enough to make it straight—and from which all lettering had long since been washed away. This cross was all that marked the abiding place of that mist-like form, so often seen at dark to stalk down the hill with threatening stride, or of moonlight nights to cross the lake in a pirogue, whose substance though visible was nought; with sound of dipping oars that made no ripple on the lake's smooth surface. On stormy nights, some more gifted with spiritual insight than their neighbors, and with hearing better sharpened to delicate intonations of the supernatural, had not only seen the mist figure mounted and flying across the hills, but had heard the panting of the blood-hounds, as the invisible pack swept by in hot pursuit of the slave so long ago at rest.

But it was "broad day," and here was nothing sinister to cause Melicent the least little thrill of awe. No owl, no bat, no ill-omened creature hovering near; only a mocking bird high up in the branches of a tall pine tree, gushing forth his shrill staccatoes as blithely as though he sang paeans to a translated soul in paradise.

"Poor old McFarlane," said Melicent, "I'll pay a little tribute to his memory; I dare say his spirit has listened to nothing but abuse of himself there in the other world, since it left his body here on the hill;" and she took one of the long-stemmed blood-red flowers and laid it beside the toppling cross.

"I reckon he's in a place w'ere flowers don't git much waterin', if they got any there."

"Shame to talk so cruelly; I don't believe in such places."

"You don't believe in hell?" he asked in blank surprise.

"Certainly not. I'm a Unitarian."

"Well, that's new to me," was his only comment.

"Do you believe in spirits, Grégoire? I don't—in day time."

"Neva mine 'bout spirits," he answered, taking her arm and leading her off, "let's git away f'om yere."

They soon found a smooth and gentle slope where Melicent sat herself comfortably down, her back against the broad support of a tree trunk, and Grégoire lay prone upon the ground with—his head in Melicent's lap.

When Melicent first met Grégoire, his peculiarities of speech, so unfamiliar to her, seemed to remove him at once from the possibility of her consideration. She was not then awake to certain fine psychological differences distinguishing man from man; precluding the possibility of naming and classifying him in the moral as one might in the animal kingdom. But short-comings of language, which finally seemed not to detract from a definite inheritance of good breeding, touched his personality as a physical deformation might, adding to it certainly no charm, yet from its pathological aspect not without a species of fascination, for a certain order of misregulated mind.

She bore with him, and then she liked him. Finally, whilst indulging in a little introspection; making a diagnosis of various symptoms, indicative by no means of a deep-seated malady, she decided that she was in love with Grégoire. But the admission embraced the understanding with herself, that nothing could come of it. She accepted it as a phase of that relentless fate which in pessimistic moments she was inclined to believe pursued her.

It could not be thought of, that she should marry a man whose eccentricity of speech would certainly not adapt itself to the requirements of polite society.

He had kissed her one day. Whatever there was about the kiss—possibly an over exuberance—it was not to her liking, and she forbade that he ever repeat it, under pain of losing her affection. Indeed, on the few occasions when Melicent had been engaged, kissing had been excluded as superfluous to the relationship, except in the case of the young lieutenant out at Fort Leavenworth who read Tennyson to her, as an angel might be supposed to read, and who in moments of rapturous self-forgetfulness, was permitted to kiss her under the ear: a proceeding not positively distasteful to Melicent, except in so much as it tickled her.

Grégoire's hair was soft, not so dark as her own, and possessed an inclination to curl about her slender fingers.

"Grégoire," she said, "you told me once that the Santien boys were a hard lot; what did you mean by that?"

"Oh no," he answered, laughing good-humoredly up into her eyes, "you did'n year me right. W'at I said was that we had a hard name in the country. I don' see w'y eitha, excep' we all'ays done putty much like we wanted. But my! a man can live like a saint yere at Place-du-Bois, they ain't no temptations o' no kine."

"There's little merit in your right doing, if you have no temptations to withstand," delivering the time worn aphorism with the air and tone of a pretty sage, giving utterance to an inspired truth.

Melicent felt that she did not fully know Grégoire; that he had always been more or less under restraint with her, and she was troubled by something other than curiosity to get at the truth concerning him. One day when she was arranging a vase of flowers at a table on the back porch, Aunt Belindy, who was scouring knives at the same table, had followed Grégoire with her glance, when he walked away after exchanging a few words with Melicent.

"God! but dats a diffunt man sence you come heah."

"Different?" questioned the girl eagerly, and casting a quick sideward look at Aunt Belindy.

"Lord yas honey, 'f you warn't heah dat same Mista Grégor 'd be in Centaville ev'y Sunday, a raisin' Cain. Humph—I knows 'im."

Melicent would not permit herself to ask more, but picked up her vase of flowers and walked with it into the house; her comprehension of Grégoire in no wise advanced by the newly acquired knowledge that he was liable to "raise Cain" during her absence—a proceeding which she could not too hastily condemn, considering her imperfect apprehension of what it might imply.

Meanwhile she would not allow her doubts to interfere with the kindness which she lavished on him, seeing that he loved her to desperation. Was he not at this very moment looking up into her eyes, and talking of his misery and her cruelty? turning his face downward in her lap—as she knew to cry—for had she not already seen him lie on the ground in an agony of tears, when she had told him he should never kiss her again?

And so they lingered in the woods, these two curious lovers, till the shadows grew so deep about old McFarlane's grave that they passed it by with hurried step and averted glance.

IX

FACE TO FACE

After a day of close and intense September heat, it had rained during the night. And now the morning had followed chill and crisp, yet with possibilities of a genial sunshine breaking through the mist that had risen at dawn from the great sluggish river and spread itself through the mazes of the city.

The change was one to send invigorating thrills through the blood, and to quicken the step; to make one like the push and jostle of the multitude that thronged the streets; to make one in love with intoxicating life, and impatient with the grudging dispensation that had given to mankind no wings wherewith to fly.

But with no reacting warmth in his heart, the change had only made Hosmer shiver and draw his coat closer about his chest, as he pushed his way through the hurrying crowd.

The St. Louis Exposition was in progress with all its many allurements that had been heralded for months through the journals of the State.

Hence, the unusual press of people on the streets this bright September morning. Home people, whose air of ownership to the surroundings classified them at once, moving unobservantly about their affairs. Women and children from the near and rich country towns, in for the Exposition and their fall shopping; wearing gowns of ultra fashionable tendencies; leaving in their toilets nothing to expediency; taking no chances of so much as a ribbon or a loop set in disaccordance with the book.

There were whole families from across the bridge, hurrying towards the Exposition. Fathers and mothers, babies and grandmothers, with baskets of lunch and bundles of provisional necessities, in for the day.

Nothing would escape their observation nor elude their criticism, from the creations in color lining the walls of the art gallery, to the most intricate mechanism of inventive genius in the basement. All would pass inspection, with drawing of comparison between the present, the past year and the "year before," likely in a nasal drawl with the R's brought sharply out, leaving no doubt as to their utterance.

The newly married couple walking serenely through the crowd, young, smiling, up-country, hand-in-hand; well pleased with themselves, with their new attire and newer jewelry, would likely have answered Hosmer's "beg pardon" with amiability if he had knocked them down. But he had only thrust them rather violently to one side in his eagerness to board the cable car that was dashing by, with no seeming willingness to stay its mad flight. He still possessed the agility in his unpracticed limbs to swing himself on the grip, where he took a front seat, well buttoned up as to top-coat, and glad of the bodily rest that his half hour's ride would bring him.

The locality in which he descended presented some noticeable changes since he had last been there. Formerly, it had been rather a quiet street, with a leisurely horse car depositing its passengers two blocks away to the north from it; awaking somewhat of afternoons when hordes of children held possession. But now the cable had come to disturb its long repose, adding in the office, nothing to its attractiveness.

There was the drug store still at the corner, with the same proprietor, tilted back in his chair as of old, and as of old reading his newspaper with only the change which a newly acquired pair of spectacles gave to his appearance. The "drug store boy" had unfolded into manhood, plainly indicated by the mustache that in adding adornment and dignity to his person, had lifted him above the menial office of window washing. A task relegated to a mustacheless urchin with a leaning towards the surreptitious abstraction of caramels and chewing gum in the intervals of such manual engagements as did not require the co-operation of a strategic mind.

Where formerly had been the vacant lot "across the street," the Sunday afternoon elysium of the youthful base ball fiend from Biddle Street, now stood a row of brand new pressed-brick "flats." Marvelous must have been the architectural ingenuity which had contrived to unite so many dwellings into so small a space. Before each spread a length of closely clipped grass plot, and every miniature front door wore its fantastic window furnishing; each set of decorations having seemingly fired the next with efforts of surpassing elaboration.

The house at which Hosmer rang—a plain two-storied red brick, standing close to the street—was very old-fashioned in face of its modern opposite neighbors, and the recently metamorphosed dwelling next door, that with added porches and appendages to tax man's faculty of conjecture, was no longer recognizable for what it had been. Even the bell which he pulled was old-fashioned and its tingle might be heard throughout the house long after the servant had opened the door, if she were only reasonably alert to the summons. Its reverberations were but dying away when Hosmer asked if Mrs. Larimore were in. Mrs. Larimore was in; an admission which seemed to hold in reserve a defiant "And what if she is, sir."

Hosmer was relieved to find the little parlor into which he was ushered, with its adjoining dining-room, much changed. The carpets which he and Fanny had gone out together to buy during the early days of their housekeeping, were replaced by rugs that lay upon the bare, well polished floors. The wall paper was different; so were the hangings. The furniture had been newly re-covered. Only the small household gods were as of old: things—trifles—that had never much occupied or impressed him, and that now, amid their altered surroundings stirred no sentiment in him of either pleased or sad remembrance.

It had not been his wish to take his wife unawares, and he had previously written her of his intended coming, yet without giving her a clue for the reason of it.

There was an element of the bull-dog in Hosmer. Having made up his mind, he indulged in no regrets, in no nursing of if's and and's, but stood like a brave soldier to his post, not a post of danger, true—but one well supplied with discomfiting possibilities.

And what had Homeyer said of it? He had railed of course as usual, at the submission of a human destiny to the exacting and ignorant rule of what he termed moral conventionalities. He had startled and angered Hosmer with his denunciation of Thérèse's sophistical guidance. Rather— he proposed—let Hosmer and Thérèse marry, and if Fanny were to be redeemed—though he pooh-poohed the notion as untenable with certain views of what he called the rights to existence: the existence of wrongs— sorrows—diseases—death—let them all go to make up the conglomerate whole—and let the individual man hold on to his personality. But if she must be redeemed—granting this point to their littleness, let the redemption come by different ways than those of sacrifice: let it be an outcome from the capability of their united happiness.

Hosmer did not listen to his friend Homeyer. Love was his god now, and Thérèse was Love's prophet.

So he was sitting in this little parlor waiting for Fanny to come.

She came after an interval that had been given over to the indulgence of a little feminine nervousness. Through the open doors Hosmer could hear her coming down the back stairs; could hear that she halted midway. Then she passed through the dining-room, and he arose and went to meet her, holding out his hand, which she was not at once ready to accept, being flustered and unprepared for his manner in whichever way it might direct itself.

They sat opposite each other and remained for a while silent; he with astonishment at sight of the "merry blue eyes" faded and sunken into deep, dark round sockets; at the net-work of little lines all traced about the mouth and eyes, and spreading over the once rounded cheeks that were now hollow and evidently pale or sallow, beneath a layer of rouge that had been laid on with an unsparing hand. Yet was she still pretty, or pleasing, especially to a strong nature that would find an appeal in the pathetic weakness of her face. There was no guessing at what her figure might be, it was disguised under a very fashionable dress, and a worsted shawl covered her shoulders, which occasionally quivered as with an inward chill. She spoke first, twisting the end of this shawl.

"What did you come for, David? why did you come now?" with peevish resistance to the disturbance of his coming.

"I know I have come without warrant," he said, answering her implication. "I have been led to see—no matter how—that I made mistakes in the past, and what I want to do now is to right them, if you will let me."

This was very unexpected to her, and it startled her, but neither with pleasure nor pain; only with an uneasiness which showed itself in her face.

"Have you been ill?" he asked suddenly as the details of change in her appearance commenced to unfold themselves to him.

"Oh no, not since last winter, when I had pneumonia so bad. They thought I was going to die. Dr. Franklin said I would 'a died if Belle Worthington hadn't 'a took such good care of me. But I don't see what you mean coming now. It'll be the same thing over again: I don't see what's the use, David."

"We won't talk about the use, Fanny. I want to take care of you for the rest of your life—or mine—as I promised to do ten years ago; and I want you to let me do it."

"It would be the same thing over again," she reiterated, helplessly.

"It will not be the same," he answered positively. "I will not be the same, and that will make all the difference needful."

"I don't see what you want to do it for, David. Why we'd haf to get married over again and all that, wouldn't we?"

"Certainly," he answered with a faint smile. "I'm living in the South now, in Louisiana, managing a sawmill down there."

"Oh, I don't like the South. I went down to Memphis, let's see, it was last spring, with Belle and Lou Dawson, after I'd been sick; and I don't see how a person can live down there."

"You would like the place where I'm living. It's a fine large plantation, and the lady who owns it would be the best of friends to you. She knew why I was coming, and told me to say she would help to make your life a happy one if she could."

"It's her told you to come," she replied in quick resentment. "I don't see what business it is of hers."

Fanny Larimore's strength of determination was not one to hold against Hosmer's will set to a purpose, during the hour or more that they talked, he proposing, she finally acquiescing. And when he left her, it was with a gathering peace in her heart to feel that his nearness was something that would belong to her again; but differently as he assured her. And she believed him, knowing that he would stand to his promise.

Her life was sometimes very blank in the intervals of street perambulations and matinées and reading of morbid literature. That elation which she had felt over her marriage with Hosmer ten years before, had soon died away, together with her weak love for him, when she began to dread him and defy him. But now that he said he was ready to take care of her and be good to her, she felt great comfort in her knowledge of his honesty.

X

Fanny's Friends

It was on the day following Hosmer's visit, that Mrs. Lorenzo Worthington, familiarly known to her friends as Belle Worthington, was occupied in constructing a careful and extremely elaborate street toilet before her dressing bureau which stood near the front window of one of the "flats" opposite Mrs. Larimore's. The Nottingham curtain screened her effectually from the view of passers-by without hindering her frequent observance of what transpired in the street.

The lower portion of this lady's figure was draped, or better, seemingly supported, by an abundance of stiffly starched white petticoats that rustled audibly at her slightest movement. Her neck was bare, as were the well shaped arms that for the past five minutes had been poised in mid-air, in the arrangement of a front of exquisitely soft blonde curls, which she had taken from her "top drawer" and was adjusting, with the aid of a multitude of tiny invisible hair-pins, to her own very smoothly brushed hair. Yellow hair it was, with a suspicious darkness about the roots, and a streakiness about the back, that to an observant eye would have more than hinted that art had assisted nature in coloring Mrs. Worthington's locks.

Dressed, and evidently waiting with forced patience for the termination of these overhead maneuvers of her friend, sat Lou,— Mrs. Jack Dawson,—a woman whom most people called handsome. If she were handsome, no one could have told why, for her beauty was a thing which could not be defined. She was tall and thin, with hair, eyes, and complexion of a brownish neutral tint, and bore in face and figure, a stamp of defiance which probably accounted for a certain eccentricity in eschewing hair dyes and cosmetics. Her face was full of little irregularities; a hardly perceptible cast in one eye; the nose drawn a bit to one side, and the mouth twitched decidedly to the other when she talked or laughed. It was this misproportion which gave a piquancy to her expression and which in charming people, no doubt made them believe her handsome.

Mrs. Worthington's coiffure being completed, she regaled herself with a deliberate and comprehensive glance into the street, and the outcome of her observation was the sudden exclamation.

"Well I'll be switched! come here quick Lou. If there ain't Fanny Larimore getting on the car with Dave Hosmer!"

Mrs. Dawson approached the window, but without haste; and in no wise sharing her friend's excitement, gave utterance to her calm opinion.

"They've made it up, I'll bet you what you want."

Surprise seemed for the moment to have deprived Mrs. Worthington of further ability to proceed with her toilet, for she had fallen into a chair as limply as her starched condition would permit, her face full of speculation.

"See here, Belle Worthington, if we've got to be at the 'Lympic at two o'clock, you'd better be getting a move on yourself."

"Yes, I know; but I declare, you might knock me down with a feather."

A highly overwrought figure of speech on the part of Mrs. Worthington, seeing that the feather which would have prostrated her must have met a resistance of some one hundred and seventy-five pounds of solid avoirdupois.

"After all she said about him, too!" seeking to draw her friend into some participation in her own dumbfoundedness.

"Well, you ought to know Fanny Larimore's a fool, don't you?"

"Well, but I just can't get over it; that's all there is about it." And Mrs. Worthington went about completing the adornment of her person in a state of voiceless stupefaction.

In full garb, she presented the figure of a splendid woman; trim and tight in a black silk gown of expensive quality, heavy with jets which hung and shone, and jangled from every available point of her person. Not a thread of her yellow hair was misplaced. She shone with cleanliness, and her broad expressionless face and meaningless blue eyes were set to a good-humored readiness for laughter, which would be wholesome if not musical. She exhaled a fragrance of patchouly or jockey-club, or something odorous and "strong" that clung to every article of her apparel, even to the yellow kid gloves which she would now be forced to put on during her ride in the car. Mrs. Dawson, attired with equal richness and style, showed more of individuality in her toilet.

As they quitted the house she observed to her friend:

"I wish you'd let up on that smell; it's enough to sicken a body."

"I know you don't like it, Lou," was Mrs. Worthington's apologetic and half disconcerted reply, "and I was careful as could be. Give you my word, I didn't think you could notice it."

"Notice it? Gee!" responded Mrs. Dawson.

These were two ladies of elegant leisure, the conditions of whose lives, and the amiability of whose husbands, had enabled them to develop into finished and professional time-killers.

Their intimacy with each other, as also their close acquaintance with Fanny Larimore, dated from a couple of years after that lady's marriage, when they had met as occupants of the same big up-town boarding house. The intercourse had never since been permitted to die out. Once, when the two former ladies were on a visit to Mrs. Larimore, seeing the flats in course of construction, they were at once assailed with the desire to abandon their hitherto nomadic life, and settle to the responsibilities of housekeeping; a scheme which they carried into effect as soon as the houses became habitable.

There was a Mr. Lorenzo Worthington; a gentleman employed for many years past in the custom house. Whether he had been overlooked, which his small unobtrusive, narrow-chested person made possible—or whether his many-sided usefulness had rendered him in a manner indispensable to his employers, does not appear; but he had remained at his post during the various changes of administration that had gone by since his first appointment.

During intervals of his work—intervals often occurring of afternoon hours, when he had been given night work—he was fond of sitting at the sunny kitchen window, with his long thin nose, and shortsighted eyes plunged between the pages of one of his precious books: a small hoard of which he had collected at some cost and more self-denial.

One of the grievances of his life was the necessity under which he found himself of protecting his treasure from the Philistine abuse and contempt of his wife. When they moved into the flat, Mrs. Worthington, during her husband's absence, had ranged them all, systematically enough, on the top shelf of the kitchen closet to "get them out of the way." But at this he had protested, and taken a positive stand, to which his wife had so far yielded as to permit that they be placed on the top shelf of the bedroom closet; averring that to have them laying around was a thing that she would not do, for they spoilt the looks of any room.

He had not foreseen the possibility of their usefulness being a temptation to his wife in so handy a receptacle.

Seeking once a volume of Ruskin's Miscellanies, he discovered that it had been employed to support the dismantled leg of a dressing bureau. On another occasion, a volume of Schopenhauer, which he had been at much difficulty and expense to procure, Emerson's Essays, and two other volumes much prized, he found had served that lady as weights to hold down a piece of dry goods which she had sponged and spread to dry on an available section of roof top.

He was glad enough to transport them all back to the safer refuge of the kitchen closet, and pay the hired girl a secret stipend to guard them.

Mr. Worthington regarded women as being of peculiar and unsuitable conformation to the various conditions of life amid which they are placed; with strong moral proclivities, for the most part subservient to a weak and inadequate mentality.

It was not his office to remodel them; his rôle was simply to endure with patience the vagaries of an order of human beings, who after all, offered an interesting study to a man of speculative habit, apart from their usefulness as propagators of the species.

As regards this last qualification, Mrs. Worthington had done less than her fair share, having but one child, a daughter of twelve, whose training and education had been assumed by an aunt of her father's, a nun of some standing in the Sacred Heart Convent.

Quite a different type of man was Jack Dawson, Lou's husband. Short, round, young, blonde, good looking and bald—as what St. Louis man past thirty is not? he rejoiced in the agreeable calling of a traveling salesman.

On the occasions when he was at home; once in two weeks— sometimes seldomer—never oftener—the small flat was turned inside out and upside down. He filled it with noise and merriment. If a theater party were not on hand, it was a spin out to Forest park behind a fast team, closing with a wine supper at a road-side restaurant. Or a card party would be hastily gathered to which such neighbors as were congenial were bid in hot haste; deficiencies being supplied from his large circle of acquaintances who happened not to be on the road, and who at the eleventh hour were rung up by telephone. On such occasions Jack's voice would be heard loud in anecdote, introduced in some such wise as "When I was in Houston, Texas, the other day," or "Tell you what it is, sir, those fellers over in Albuquerque are up to a thing or two."

One of his standing witticisms was to inquire in a stage whisper of Belle or Lou—whether the little gal over the way had taken the pledge yet.

This gentleman and his wife were on the most amiable of terms together, barring the small grievance that he sometimes lost money at poker. But as losing was exceptional with him, and as he did not

KATE CHOPIN

make it a matter of conscience to keep her at all times posted as to the fluctuations of his luck, this grievance had small occasion to show itself.

What he thought of his wife, might best be told in his own language: that Lou was up to the mark and game every time; feminine characteristics which he apparently held in high esteem.

The two ladies in question had almost reached the terminus of their ride, when Mrs. Worthington remarked incidentally to her friend, "It was nothing in the God's world but pure sass brought those two fellers to see you last night, Lou."

Mrs. Dawson bit her lip and the cast in her eye became more accentuated, as it was apt to do when she was ruffled.

"I notice you didn't treat 'em any too cool yourself," she retorted.

"Oh, they weren't my company, or I'd a give 'em a piece of my mind pretty quick. You know they're married, and they know you're married, and they hadn't a bit o' business there."

"They're perfect gentlemen, and I don't see what business 'tis of yours, anyway."

"Oh that's a horse of another color," replied Mrs. Worthington, bridling and relapsing into injured silence for the period of ten seconds, when she resumed, "I hope they ain't going to poke themselves at the matinée."

"Likely they will 's long as they gave us the tickets."

One of the gentlemen was at the matinée: Mr. Bert Rodney, but he certainly had not "poked" himself there. He never did any thing vulgar or in bad taste. He had only "dropped in!" Exquisite in dress and manner, a swell of the upper circles, versed as was no one better in the code of gentlemanly etiquette—he was for the moment awaiting disconsolately the return of his wife and daughter from Narragansett.

He took a vacant seat behind the two ladies, and bending forward began to talk to them in his low and fascinating drawl.

Mrs. Worthington, who often failed to accomplish her fierce designs, was as gracious towards him as if she had harbored no desire to give him a piece of her mind; but she was resolute in her refusal to make one of a proposed supper party.

A quiet sideward look from Mrs. Dawson, told Mr. Rodney as plainly as words, that in the event of his *partie-carrée* failing him, he might count upon her for a *tête-à-tête*.

XI

The Self-Assumed Burden

The wedding was over. Hosmer and Fanny had been married in the small library of their Unitarian minister whom they had found intent upon the shaping of his Sunday sermon.

Out of deference, he had been briefly told the outward circumstances of the case, which he knew already; for these two had been formerly members of his congregation, and gossip had not been reluctant in telling their story. Hosmer, of course, had drifted away from his knowledge, and in late years, he had seen little of Fanny, who when moved to attend church at all usually went to the Redemptorist's Rock Church with her friend Belle Worthington. This lady was a good Catholic to the necessary extent of hearing a mass on Sundays, abstaining from meat on Fridays and Ember days, and making her "Easters." Which concessions were not without their attendant discomforts, counterbalanced, however, by the soothing assurance which they gave her of keeping on the safe side.

The minister had been much impressed with the significance of this re-marriage which he was called upon to perform, and had offered some few and well chosen expressions of salutary advice as to its future guidance. The sexton and housekeeper had been called in as witnesses. Then Hosmer had taken Fanny back home in a cab as she requested, because of her eyes that were red and swollen.

Inside the little hall-way he took her in his arms and kissed her, calling her "my child." He could not have told why, except that it expressed the responsibility he accepted of bearing all things that a father must bear from the child to whom he has given life.

"I should like to go out for an hour, Fanny; but if you would rather not, I shall stay."

"No, David, I want to be alone," she said, turning into the little parlor, with eyes big and heavy from weariness and inward clashing emotions.

Along the length of Lindell avenue from Grand avenue west to Forest park, reaches for two miles on either side of the wide and well kept gravel drive a smooth stone walk, bordered its full extent with a double row of trees which were young and still uncertain, when Hosmer walked between them.

Had it been Sunday, he would have found himself making one of a fashionable throng of promenaders; it being at that time a fad with society people to walk to Forest park and back of a Sunday afternoon. Driving was then considered a respectable diversion only on the six work days of the week.

But it was not Sunday and this inviting promenade was almost deserted. An occasional laborer would walk clumsily by; apathetic; swinging his tin bucket and bearing some implement of toil with the yellow clay yet clinging to it. Or it might be a brace of strong-minded girls walking with long and springing stride, which was then fashionable; looking not to the right nor left; indulging in no exchange of friendly and girlish chatter, but grimly intent upon the purpose of their walk.

A steady line of vehicles was pushing on towards the park at the moderate speed which the law required. On both sides the wide boulevard tasteful dwellings, many completed, but most of them in course of construction, were in constant view. Hosmer noted every thing, but absently; and yet he was not pre-occupied with thought. He felt himself to be hurrying away from something that was fast overtaking him, and his faculties for the moment were centered in the mere act of motion. It is said that motion is pleasurable to man. No doubt, in connection with a healthy body and free mind, movement brings to the normal human being a certain degree of enjoyment. But where the healthful conditions are only physical, rapid motion changes from a source of pleasure to one of mere expediency.

So long as Hosmer could walk he kept a certain pressing consciousness at bay. He would have liked to run if he had dared. Since he had entered the park there were constant trains of cars speeding somewhere overhead; he could hear them at near intervals clashing over the stone bridge. And there was not a train which passed that he did not long to be at the front of it to measure and let out its speed. What a mad flight he would have given it, to make men hold their breath with terror! How he would have driven it till its end was death and chaos!— so much the better.

There suddenly formed in Hosmer's mind a sentence—sharp and distinct. We are all conscious of such quick mental visions whether of words or pictures, coming sometimes from a hidden and untraceable source, making us quiver with awe at this mysterious power of mind manifesting itself with the vividness of visible matter.

"It was the act of a coward."

Those were the words which checked him, and forbade him to go farther: which compelled him to turn about and face the reality of his convictions.

It is no unusual sight, that of a man lying full length in the soft tender grass of some retired spot of Forest park—with his face hidden in his folded arms. To the few who may see him, if they speculate at all about him he sleeps or he rests his body after a day's fatigue. "Am I never to be the brave man?" thought Hosmer, "always the coward, flying even from my own thoughts?"

How hard to him was this unaccustomed task of dealing with moral difficulties, which all through his life before, however lightly they had come, he had shirked and avoided! He realized now, that there was to be no more of that. If he did not wish his life to end in disgraceful shipwreck, he must take command and direction of it upon himself.

He had felt himself capable of stolid endurance since love had declared itself his guide and helper. But now—only to-day—something beside had crept into his heart. Not something to be endured, but a thing to be strangled and thrust away. It was the demon of hate; so new, so awful, so loathsome, he doubted that he could look it in the face and live.

Here was the problem of his new existence.

The woman who had formerly made his life colorless and empty he had quietly turned his back upon, carrying with him a pity that was not untender. But the woman who had unwittingly robbed him of all possibility of earthly happiness—he hated her. The woman who for the remainder of a life-time was to be in all the world the nearest thing to him, he hated her. He hated this woman of whom he must be careful, to whom he must be tender, and loyal and generous. And to give no sign or word but of kindness; to do no action that was not considerate, was the task which destiny had thrust upon his honor.

He did not ask himself if it were possible of accomplishment. He had flung hesitancy away, to make room for the all-powerful "Must be."

He walked slowly back to his home. There was no need to run now; nothing pursued him. Should he quicken his pace or drag himself ever so slowly, it could henceforth make no difference. The burden from which he had fled was now banded upon him and not to be loosed, unless he fling himself with it into forgetfulness.

XII

Severing Old Ties

Returning from the matinée, Belle and her friend Lou Dawson, before entering their house, crossed over to Fanny's. Mrs. Worthington tried the door and finding it fastened, rang the bell, then commenced to beat a tattoo upon the pane with her knuckles; an ingenuous manner which she had of announcing her identity. Fanny opened to them herself, and the three walked into the parlor.

"I haven't seen you for a coon's age, Fanny," commenced Belle, "where on earth have you been keeping yourself?"

"You saw me yesterday breakfast time, when you came to borrow the wrapper pattern," returned Fanny, in serious resentment to her friend's exaggeration.

"And much good the old wrapper pattern did me: a mile too small every way, no matter how much I let out the seams. But see here—"

"Belle's the biggest idiot about her size: there's no convincing her she's not a sylph."

"*Thank* you, Mrs. Dawson."

"Well, it's a fact. Didn't you think Furgeson's scales were all wrong the other day because you weighed a hundred and eighty pounds?"

"O that's the day I had that heavy rep on."

"Heavy nothing. We were coming over last night, Fanny, but we had company," continued Mrs. Dawson.

"Who d'you have?" asked Fanny mechanically and glad of the respite.

"Bert Rodney and Mr. Grant. They're so anxious to meet you. I'd 'a sent over for you, but Belle—"

"See here, Fanny, what the mischief was Dave Hosmer doing here to-day, and going down town with you and all that sort o' thing?"

Fanny flushed uneasily. "Have you seen the evening paper?" she asked.

"How d'you want us to see the paper? we just come from the matinée."

"David came yesterday," Fanny said working nervously at the window shade. "He'd wrote me a note the postman brought right after you left with the pattern. When you saw us getting on the car, we were going down to Dr. Martin's, and we've got married again."

Mrs. Dawson uttered a long, low whistle by way of comment. Mrs. Worthington gave vent to her usual "Well I'll be switched," which she was capable of making expressive of every shade of astonishment, from the lightest to the most pronounced; at the same time unfastening the bridle of her bonnet which plainly hindered her free respiration after such a shock.

"Say that Fanny isn't sly, after that, Belle."

"Sly? My God, she's a fool! If ever a woman had a snap! and to go to work and let a man get around her like that."

Mrs. Worthington seemed powerless to express herself in anything but disconnected exclamations.

"What are you going to do, Fanny?" asked Lou, who having aired all the astonishment which she cared to show, in her whistle, was collected enough to want her natural curiosity satisfied.

"David's living down South. I guess we'll go down there pretty soon. Soon's he can get things fixed up here."

"Where—down South?"

"Oh, I don't know. Somewheres in Louisiana."

"It's to be hoped in New Orleans," spoke Belle didactically, "that's the only decent place in Louisiana where a person could live."

"No, 'tain't in New Orleans. He's got a saw mill somewheres down there."

"Heavens and earth! a saw mill?" shrieked Belle. Lou was looking calmly resigned to the startling news.

"Oh, I ain't going to live in a saw mill. I wisht you'd all let me alone, any way," she returned pettishly. "There's a lady keeps a plantation, and that's where he lives."

"Well of all the rigmaroles! a lady, and a saw mill and a plantation. It's my opinion that man could make you believe black's white, Fanny Larimore."

As Hosmer approached his house, he felt mechanically in his pocket for his latch key; so small a trick having come back to him with the old habit of misery. Of course he found no key. His ring startled Fanny, who at once sprang from her seat to open the door for him; but having taken a few steps, she hesitated and irresolutely re-seated herself. It was only his second ring that the servant unamiably condescended to answer.

"So you're going to take Fanny away from us, Mr. Hosmer," said Belle, when he had greeted them and seated himself beside Mrs. Dawson on the small sofa that stood between the door and window. Fanny sat at the adjoining window, and Mrs. Worthington in the center of the room; which was indeed so small a room that any one of them might have reached out and almost touched the hand of the others.

"Yes, Fanny has agreed to go South with me," he answered briefly. "You're looking well, Mrs. Worthington."

"Oh, Law yes, I'm never sick. As I tell Mr. Worthington, he'll never get rid of me, unless he hires somebody to murder me. But I tell you what, you came pretty near not having any Fanny to take away with you. She was the sickest woman! Did you tell him about it, Fanny? Come to think of it, I guess the climate down there'll be the very thing to bring her round."

Mrs. Dawson without offering apology interrupted her friend to inquire of Hosmer if his life in the South were not of the most interesting, and begging that he detail them something of it; with a look to indicate that she felt the deepest concern in anything that touched him.

A masculine presence had always the effect of rousing Mrs. Dawson into an animation which was like the glow of a slumbering ember, when a strong pressure of air is brought to bear upon it.

Hosmer had always considered her an amiable woman, with rather delicate perceptions; frivolous, but without the vulgarisms of Mrs. Worthington, and consequently a less objectionable friend for Fanny. He answered, looking down into her eyes, which were full of attentiveness.

"My life in the South is not one that you would think interesting. I live in the country where there are no distractions such as you ladies call amusements—and I work pretty hard. But it's the sort of life that one grows attached to and finds himself longing for again if he have occasion to change it."

"Yes, it must be very satisfying," she answered; for the moment perfectly sincere.

"Oh very!" exclaimed Mrs. Worthington, with a loud and aggressive laugh. "It would just suit you to a T, Lou, but how it's going to satisfy Fanny! Well, I've got nothing to say about it, thanks be; it don't concern me."

"If Fanny finds that she doesn't like it after a fair trial, she has the privilege of saying so, and we shall come back again," he said looking at his wife whose elevation of eyebrow, and droop of mouth gave her the expression of martyred resignation, which St. Lawrence might have worn, when invited to make himself comfortable on the gridiron—so had Mrs. Worthington's words impressed her with the force of their prophetic meaning.

Mrs. Dawson politely hoped that Hosmer would not leave before Jack came home; it would distress Jack beyond everything to return and find that he had missed an old friend whom he thought so much of.

Hosmer could not say precisely when they would leave. He was in present negotiation with a person who wanted to rent the house, furnished; and just as soon as he could arrange a few business details, and Fanny could gather such belongings as she wished to take with her they would go.

"You seem mighty struck on Dave Hosmer, all of a sudden," remarked Mrs. Worthington to her friend, as the two crossed over the street. "A feller without any more feelings than a stick; it's what I always said about him."

"Oh, I always did like Hosmer," replied Mrs. Dawson. "But I thought he had more sense than to tie himself to that little gump again, after he'd had the luck to get rid of her."

A few days later Jack came home. His return was made palpable to the entire neighborhood; for no cab ever announced itself with quite the dash and clatter and bang of door that Jack's cabs did.

The driver had staggered behind him under the weight of the huge yellow valise, and had been liberally paid for the service.

Immediately the windows were thrown wide open, and the lace curtains drawn aside until no smallest vestige of them remained visible from the street. A condition of things which Mrs. Worthington upstairs bitterly resented, and naturally, spoiling as it necessarily did, the general *coup d'œil* of the flat to passers-by. But Mrs. Dawson had won her husband's esteem by just such acts as this one of amiable permission to ventilate the house according to methods of his own and essentially masculine; regardless of dust that might be flying, or sun that might be shining with disastrous results to the parlor carpet.

Clouds of tobacco smoke were seen to issue from the open windows. Those neighbors whose openings commanded a view of the Dawson's alley-gate might have noted the hired girl starting for the grocery with unusual animation of step, and returning with her basket well stocked with beer and soda bottles—a provision made against a need for "dutch-cocktails," likely to assail Jack during his hours of domesticity.

In the evening the same hired girl, breathless from the multiplicity of errands which she had accomplished during the day, appeared at the Hosmers with a message that Mrs. Dawson wanted them to "come over."

They were preparing to leave on the morrow, but concluded that they could spare a few moments in which to bid adieu to their friends.

Jack met them at the very threshold, with warm and hearty hand-shaking, and loud protest when he learned that they had not come to spend the evening and that they were going away next day.

"Great Scott! you're not leaving to-morrow? And I ain't going to have a chance to get even with Mrs. Hosmer on that last deal? By Jove, she knows how to do it," he said, addressing Hosmer and holding Fanny familiarly by the elbow. "Drew to the middle, sir, and hang me, if she didn't fill. Takes a woman to do that sort o' thing; and me a laying for her with three aces. Hello there, girls! here's Hosmer and Fanny," in response to which summons his wife and Mrs. Worthington issued from the depths of the dining-room, where they had been engaged in preparing certain refreshments for the expected guests.

"See here, Lou, we'll have to fix it up some way to go and see them off to-morrow. If you'd manage to lay over till Thursday I could join you as far as Little Rock. But no, that's a fact," he added reflectively, "I've got to be in Cincinnati on Thursday."

They had all entered the parlor, and Mrs. Worthington suggested that Hosmer go up and make a visit to her husband, whom he would find up there "poring over those everlasting books."

"I don't know what's got into Mr. Worthington lately," she said, "he's getting that religious. If it ain't the Bible he's poring over, well it's something or other just as bad."

The brightly burning light guided Hosmer to the kitchen, where he found Lorenzo Worthington seated beside his student lamp at the table, which was covered with a neat red cloth. On the gas-stove was spread a similar cloth and the floor was covered with a shining oil-cloth.

Mr. Worthington was startled, having already forgotten that his wife had told him of Hosmer's return to St. Louis.

"Why, Mr. Hosmer, is this you? come, come into the parlor, this is no place," shaking Hosmer's hand and motioning towards the parlor.

"No, it's very nice and cozy here, and I have only a moment to stay," said Hosmer, seating himself beside the table on which the other had laid his book, with his spectacles between the pages to mark his place.

Mr. Worthington then did a little hemming and hawing preparatory to saying something fitting the occasion; not wishing to be hasty in offering the old established form of congratulation, in a case whose peculiarity afforded him no precedential guide. Hosmer came to his relief by observing quite naturally that he and his wife had come over to say good-bye, before leaving for the South, adding "no doubt Mrs. Worthington has told you."

"Yes, yes, and I'm sure we're very sorry to lose you; that is, Mrs. Larimore—I should say Mrs. Hosmer. Isabella will certainly regret her departure, I see them always together, you know."

"You cling to your old habit, I see, Mr. Worthington," said Hosmer, indicating his meaning by a motion of the hand towards the book on the table.

"Yes, to a certain extent. Always within the forced limits, you understand. At this moment I am much interested in tracing the history of various religions which are known to us; those which have died out, as well as existing religions. It is curious, indeed, to note the circumstances of their birth, their progress and inevitable death; seeming to follow the course of nations in such respect. And the similitude which stamps them all, is also a feature worthy of study. You would perhaps be surprised, sir, to discover the points of resemblance which indicate in them a common origin. To observe the slight differences, indeed technical differences, distinguishing the Islam from the Hebrew, or both from the Christian religion. The creeds are obviously ramifications from the one deep-rooted trunk which we call religion. Have you ever thought of this, Mr. Hosmer?"

"No, I admit that I've not gone into it. Homeyer would have me think that all religions are but mythological creations invented to satisfy a species of sentimentality—a morbid craving in man for the unknown and undemonstrable."

"That is where he is wrong; where I must be permitted to differ from him. As you would find, my dear sir, by following carefully the history of mankind, that the religious sentiment is implanted, a true and legitimate attribute of the human soul—with peremptory right to its existence. Whatever may be faulty in the creeds—that makes no difference, the foundation is there and not to be dislodged. Homeyer, as I understand him from your former not infrequent references, is an Iconoclast, who would tear down and leave devastation behind him; building up nothing. He would deprive a clinging humanity of the supports about which she twines herself, and leave her helpless and sprawling upon the earth."

"No, no, he believes in a natural adjustment," interrupted Hosmer. "In an innate reserve force of accommodation. What we commonly call laws in nature, he styles accidents—in society, only arbitrary methods of expediency, which, when they outlive their usefulness to an advancing and exacting civilization, should be set aside. He is a little impatient to always wait for the inevitable natural adjustment."

"Ah, my dear Mr. Hosmer, the world is certainly to-day not prepared to stand the lopping off and wrenching away of old traditions. She must take her stand against such enemies of the conventional. Take religion away from the life of man—"

"Well, I knew it—I was just as sure as preaching," burst out Mrs. Worthington, as she threw open the door and confronted the two men—resplendent in "baby blue" and much steel ornamentation. "As I tell Mr. Worthington, he ought to turn Christian Brother or something and be done with it."

"No, no, my dear; Mr. Hosmer and I have merely been interchanging a few disjointed ideas."

"I'll be bound they were disjointed. I guess Fanny wants you, Mr. Hosmer. If you listen to Mr. Worthington he'll keep you here till daylight with his ideas."

Hosmer followed Mrs. Worthington down-stairs and into Mrs. Dawson's. As he entered the parlor he heard Fanny laughing gaily, and saw that she stood near the sideboard in the dining-room, just clicking her glass of punch to Jack Dawson's, who was making a gay speech on the occasion of her new marriage.

They did not leave when they had intended. Need the misery of that one day be told?

But on the evening of the following day, Fanny peered with pale, haggard face from the closed window of the Pullman car as it moved slowly out of Union depôt, to see Lou and Jack Dawson smiling and waving good-bye, Belle wiping her eyes and Mr. Worthington looking blankly along the line of windows, unable to see them without his spectacles, which he had left between the pages of his Schopenhauer on the kitchen table at home.

I

FANNY'S FIRST NIGHT AT PLACE-DU-BOIS

The journey South had not been without attractions for Fanny. She had that consciousness so pleasing to the feminine mind of being well dressed; for her husband had been exceedingly liberal in furnishing her the means to satisfy her fancy in that regard. Moreover the change holding out a promise of novelty, irritated her to a feeble expectancy. The air, that came to her in puffs through the car window, was deliciously soft and mild; steeped with the rich languor of the Indian summer, that had already touched the tree tops, the sloping hill-side, and the very air, with russet and gold.

Hosmer sat beside her, curiously inattentive to his newspaper; observant of her small needs, and anticipating her timid half expressed wishes. Was there some mysterious power that had so soon taught the man such methods to a woman's heart, or was he not rather on guard and schooling himself for the rôle which was to be acted out to the end? But as the day was approaching its close, Fanny became tired and languid; a certain mistrust was creeping into her heart with the nearing darkness. It had grown sultry and close, and the view from the car window was no longer cheerful, as they whirled through forests, gloomy with trailing moss, or sped over an unfamiliar country whose features were strange and held no promise of a welcome for her.

They were nearing Place-du-Bois, and Hosmer's spirits had risen almost to the point of gaiety as he began to recognize the faces of those who loitered about the stations at which they stopped. At the Centerville station, five miles before reaching their own, he had even gone out on the platform to shake hands with the rather mystified agent who had not known of his absence. And he had waved a salute to the little French priest of Centerville who stood out in the open beside his horse, booted, spurred and all equipped for bad weather, waiting for certain consignments which were to come with the train, and who answered Hosmer's greeting with a sober and uncompromising sweep of the hand. When the whistle sounded for Place-du-Bois, it was nearly dark. Hosmer hurried Fanny on to the platform, where stood Henry, his clerk. There were a great many negroes loitering about, some of whom offered him a cordial "how'dy Mr. Hosma," and pushing through was Grégoire, meeting them with the ease of a courtier, and acknowledging Hosmer's introduction of his wife, with a friendly hand shake.

"Aunt Thérèse sent the buggy down fur you," he said, "we had rain this mornin' and the road's putty heavy. Come this way. Mine out fur that ba'el, Mrs. Hosma, it's got molasses in. Hiurm bring that buggy ova yere."

"What's the news, Grégoire?" asked Hosmer, as they waited for Hiram to turn the horses about.

"Jus' about the same's ev'a. Miss Melicent wasn't ver' well a few days back; but she's some betta. I reckon you're all plum wore out," he added, taking in Fanny's listless attitude, and thinking her very pretty as far as he could discover in the dim light.

They drove directly to the cottage, and on the porch Thérèse was waiting for them. She took Fanny's two hands and pressed them warmly between her own; then led her into the house with an arm passed about her waist. She shook hands with Hosmer, and stood for a while in cheerful conversation, before leaving them.

The cottage was fully equipped for their reception, with Minervy in possession of the kitchen and the formerly reluctant Suze as housemaid: though Thérèse had been silent as to the methods which she had employed to prevail with these unwilling damsels.

Hosmer then went out to look after their baggage, and when he returned, Fanny sat with her head pillowed on the sofa, sobbing bitterly. He knelt beside her, putting his arm around her, and asked the cause of her distress.

"Oh it's so lonesome, and dreadful, I don't believe I can stand it," she answered haltingly through her tears.

And here was he thinking it was so home-like and comforting, and tasting the first joy that he had known since he had gone away.

"It's all strange and new to you, Fanny; try to bear up for a day or two. Come now, don't be a baby—take courage. It will all seem quite different by and by, when the sun shines."

A knock at the door was followed by the entrance of a young colored boy carrying an armful of wood.

"Miss T'rèse sont me kin'le fiar fu' Miss Hosma; 'low he tu'nin' cole," he said depositing his load on the hearth; and Fanny, drying her eyes, turned to watch him at his work.

He went very deliberately about it, tearing off thin slathers from the fat pine, and arranging them into a light frame-work, beneath a topping of kindling and logs that he placed on the massive brass andirons. He crawled about on hands and knees, picking up the stray bits of chips and moss that had fallen from his arms when he came in. Then sitting back on his heels he looked meditatively into the blaze which he had kindled and scratched his nose with a splinter of pine wood. When Hosmer presently left the room, he rolled his big black eyes towards Fanny, without turning his head, and remarked in a tone plainly inviting conversation "yo' all come f'om way yonda?"

He was intensely black, and if Fanny had been a woman with the slightest sense of humor, she could not but have been amused at the picture which he presented in the revealing fire-light with his elfish and ape like body much too small to fill out the tattered and ill-fitting garments that hung about it. But she only wondered at him and his rags, and at his motive for addressing her.

"We're come from St. Louis," she replied, taking him with a seriousness which in no wise daunted him.

"Yo' all brung de rain," he went on sociably, leaving off the scratching of his nose, to pass his black yellow-palmed hand slowly through the now raging fire, a feat which filled her with consternation. After prevailing upon him to desist from this salamander like exhibition, she was moved to ask if he were not very poor to be thus shabbily clad.

"No 'um," he laughed, "I got some sto' close yonda home. Dis yere coat w'at Mista Grégor gi'me," looking critically down at its length, which swept the floor as he remained on his knees. "He done all to'e tu pieces time he gi' him tu me, whar he scuffle wid Joçint yonda tu de mill. Mammy 'low she gwine mek him de same like new w'en she kin kotch de time."

The entrance of Minervy bearing a tray temptingly arranged with a dainty supper, served to silence the boy, who at seeing her, threw himself upon all fours and appeared to be busy with the fire. The woman, a big raw-boned field hand, set her burden awkwardly down on a table, and after staring comprehensively around, addressed the boy in a low rich voice, "Dar ain't no mo' call to bodda wid dat fiar, you Sampson; how come Miss T'rèse sont you lazy piece in yere tu buil' fiar?"

"Don' know how come," he replied, vanishing with an air of the utmost self-depreciation.

Hosmer and Fanny took tea together before the cheerful fire and he told her something of methods on the plantation, and made her further acquainted with the various people whom she had thus far encountered.

She listened apathetically; taking little interest in what he said, and asking few questions. She did express a little bewilderment at the servant problem. Mrs. Lafirme, during their short conversation, had deplored her inability to procure more than two servants for her; and Fanny could not understand why it should require so many to do the work which at home was accomplished by one. But she was tired—very tired, and early sought her bed, and Hosmer went in quest of his sister whom he had not yet seen.

Melicent had been told of his marriage some days previously, and had been thrown into such a state of nerves by the intelligence, as to seriously alarm those who surrounded her and whose experience with hysterical girls had been inadequate.

Poor Grégoire had betaken himself with the speed of the wind to the store to procure bromide, valerian, and whatever else should be thought available in prevailing with a malady of this distressing nature. But she was "some betta," as he told Hosmer, who found her walking in the darkness of one of the long verandas, all enveloped in filmy white wool. He was a little prepared for a cool reception from her, and ten minutes before she might have received him with a studied indifference. But her mood had veered about and touched the point which moved her to fall upon his neck, and in a manner, condole with him; seasoning her sympathy with a few tears.

"Whatever possessed you, David? I have been thinking, and thinking, and I can see no reason which should have driven you to do this thing. Of course I can't meet her; you surely don't expect it?"

He took her arm and joined her in her slow walk.

"Yes, I do expect it, Melicent, and if you have the least regard for me, I expect more. I want you to be good to her, and patient, and show yourself her friend. No one can do such things more amiably than you, when you try."

"But David, I had hoped for something so different."

"You couldn't have expected me to marry Mrs. Lafirme, a Catholic," he said, making no pretense of misunderstanding her.

"I think that woman would have given up religion—anything for you."

"Then you don't know her, little sister."

It must have been far in the night when Fanny awoke suddenly. She could not have told whether she had been awakened by the long, wailing cry of a traveler across the narrow river, vainly trying to rouse the ferryman; or the creaking of a heavy wagon that labored slowly by in the road and moved Hector to noisy enquiry. Was it not rather the pattering rain that the wind was driving against the window panes? The lamp burned dimly upon the high old-fashioned mantel-piece and her husband had thoughtfully placed an improvised screen before it, to protect her against its disturbance. He himself was not beside her, nor was he in the room. She slid from her bed and moved softly on her bare feet over to the open sitting-room door.

The fire had all burned away. Only the embers lay in a glowing heap, and while she looked, the last stick that lay across the andirons, broke through its tapering center and fell amongst them, stirring a fitful light by which she discovered her husband seated and bowed like a man who has been stricken. Uncomprehending, she stood a moment speechless, then crept back noiselessly to bed.

II

"Neva to See You!"

Thérèse judged it best to leave Fanny a good deal to herself during her first days on the plantation, without relinquishing a certain watchful supervision of her comfort, and looking in on her for a few moments each day. The rain which had come with them continued fitfully and Fanny remained in doors, clad in a warm handsome gown, her small slippered feet cushioned before the fire, and reading the latest novel of one of those prolific female writers who turn out their unwholesome intellectual sweets so tirelessly, to be devoured by the girls and women of the age.

Melicent, who always did the unexpected, crossed over early on the morning after Fanny's arrival; penetrated to her sleeping room and embraced her effusively, even as she lay in bed, calling her "poor dear Fanny" and cautioning her against getting up on such a morning.

The tears which had come to Fanny on arriving, and which had dried on her cheek when she turned to gaze into the cheer of the great wood fire, did not return. Everybody seemed to be making much of her, which was a new experience in her life; she having always felt herself as of little consequence, and in a manner, overlooked. The negroes were overawed at the splendor of her toilettes and showed a respect for her in proportion to the money value which these toilettes reflected. Each morning Grégoire left at her door his compliments with a huge bouquet of brilliant and many colored crysanthemums, and enquiry if he could serve her in any way. And Hosmer's time, that was not given to work, was passed at her side; not in brooding or pre-occupied silence, but in talk that invited her to friendly response.

With Thérèse, she was at first shy and diffident, and over watchful of herself. She did not forget that Hosmer had told her "The lady knows why I have come" and she resented that knowledge which Thérèse possessed of her past intimate married life.

Melicent's attentions did not last in their ultra-effusiveness, but she found Fanny less objectionable since removed from her St. Louis surroundings; and the evident consideration with which she had been accepted at Place-du-Bois seemed to throw about her a halo of sufficient distinction to impel the girl to view her from a new and different standpoint.

But the charm of plantation life was letting go its hold upon Melicent. Grégoire's adoration alone, and her feeble response to it were all that kept her.

"I neva felt anything like this befo'," he said, as they stood together and their hands touched in reaching for a splendid rose that hung invitingly from its tall latticed support out in mid lawn. The sun had come again and dried the last drop of lingering moisture on grass and shrubbery.

"W'en I'm away f'om you, even fur five minutes, 't seems like I mus' hurry quick, quick, to git back again; an' w'en I'm with you, everything 'pears all right, even if you don't talk to me or look at me. Th' otha day, down at the gin," he continued, "I was figurin' on some weights an' wasn't thinkin' about you at all, an' all at once I remember'd the one time I'd kissed you. Goodness! I couldn't see the figures any mo', my head swum and the pencil mos' fell out o' my han'. I neva felt anything like it: hones', Miss Melicent, I thought I was goin' to faint fur a minute."

"That's very unwise, Grégoire," she said, taking the roses that he handed her to add to the already large bunch. "You must learn to think of me calmly: our love must be something like a sacred memory—a sweet recollection to help us through life when we are apart."

"I don't know how I'm goin' to stan' it. Neva to see you! neva—my God!" he gasped, paling and crushing between his nervous fingers the flower she would have taken from him.

"There is nothing in this world that one cannot grow accustomed to, dear," spoke the pretty philosopher, picking up her skirts daintily with one hand and passing the other through his arm—the hand which held the flowers, whose peculiar perfume ever afterwards made Grégoire shiver through a moment of pain that touched very close upon rapture.

He was more occupied than he liked during those busy days of harvesting and ginning, that left him only brief and snatched intervals of Melicent's society. If he could have rested in the comfort of being sure of her, such moments of separation would have had their compensation in reflective anticipation. But with his undisciplined desires and hot-blooded eagerness, her half-hearted acknowledgments and inadequate concessions, closed her about with a chilling barrier that staggered him with its problematic nature. Feeling himself her equal in the aristocracy of blood, and her master in the knowledge and strength of loving, he resented those half understood reasons which removed him from the possibility of being anything to her. And more, he was angry with himself for acquiescing in that self understood agreement. But it was only in her absence that these thoughts disturbed him. When he was with her, his whole being rejoiced in her existence and there was no room for doubt or dread.

He felt himself regenerated through love, and as having no part in that other Grégoire whom he only thought of to dismiss with unrecognition.

The time came when he could ill conceal his passion from others. Thérèse became conscious of it, through an unguarded glance. The unhappiness of the situation was plain to her; but to what degree she could not guess. It was certainly so deplorable that it would have been worth while to have averted it. Yet, she felt great faith in the power of time and absence to heal such wounds even to the extent of leaving no tell-tale scar.

"Grégoire, my boy," she said to him, speaking in French, and laying her hand on his, when they were alone together. "I hope that your heart is not too deep in this folly."

He reddened and asked, "What do you mean, aunt?"

"I mean, that unfortunately, you are in love with Melicent. I do not know how much longer she will remain here, but taking any possibility for granted, let me advise you to leave the place for a while; go back to your home, or take a little trip to the city."

"No, I could not."

"Force yourself to it."

"And lose days, perhaps weeks, of being near her? No, no, I could not do that, aunt. There will be plenty time for that in the rest of my life," he said, trying to speak calmly and forcing his voice to a harshness which the nearness of tears made needful.

"Does she know? Have you told her?"

"Oh yes, she knows how much I love her."

"And she does not love you," said Thérèse, seeming rather to assert than to question.

"No, she does not. No matter what she says—she does not. I can feel that here," he answered, striking his breast. "Oh aunt, it is terrible to think of her going away; forever, perhaps; of never seeing her. I could not stand it." And he stood the strain no longer, but sobbed and wept with his aunt's consoling arms around him.

Thérèse, knowing that Melicent would not tarry much longer with them, thought it not needful to approach her on the subject. Had it been otherwise, she would not have hesitated to beg the girl to desist from this unprofitable amusement of tormenting a human heart.

III

A Talk Under the Cedar Tree

Day by day, Fanny threw off somewhat of the homesickness which had weighted her at coming. Not by any determined effort of the will, nor by any resolve to make the best of things. Outside influences meeting half-way the workings of unconscious inward forces, were the agents that by degrees were gently ridding her of the acute pressure of dissatisfaction, which up to the present, she had stolidly borne without any personal effort to cast it off.

Thérèse affected her forcibly. This woman so wholesome, so fair and strong; so un-American as to be not ashamed to show tenderness and sympathy with eye and lip, moved Fanny like a new and pleasing experience. When Thérèse touched her caressingly, or gently stroked her limp hand, she started guiltily, and looked furtively around to make sure that none had witnessed an exhibition of tenderness that made her flush, and the first time found her unresponsive. A second time, she awkwardly returned the hand pressure, and later, these mildly sensuous exchanges prefaced the outpouring of all Fanny's woes, great and small.

"I don't say that I always done what was right, Mrs. Laferm, but I guess David's told you just what suited him about me. You got to remember there's always two sides to a story."

She had been to the poultry yard with Thérèse, who had introduced her to its feathery tenants, making her acquainted with stately Brahmas and sleek Plymouth-Rocks and hardy little "Creole chickens"—not much to look at, but very palatable when converted into *fricassée*.

Returning, they seated themselves on the bench that encircled a massive cedar—spreading and conical. Hector, who had trotted attendance upon them during their visit of inspection, cast himself heavily down at his mistress' feet and after glancing knowingly up into her face, looked placidly forth at Sampson, gathering garden greens on the other side of a low dividing fence.

"You see if David'd always been like he is now, I don't know but things'd been different. Do you suppose he ever went any wheres with me, or even so much as talked to me when he came home? There was always that everlasting newspaper in his pocket, and he'd haul it out the first thing. Then I used to read the paper too sometimes, and when I'd go to talk to him about what I read, he'd never even looked at the same things. Goodness knows what he read in the paper, I never could find out; but here'd be the edges all covered over with figuring. I believe it's the only thing he ever thought or dreamt about; that eternal figuring on every bit of paper he could lay hold of, till I was tired picking them up all over the house. Belle Worthington used to say it'd of took an angel to stand him. I mean his throwing papers around that way. For as far as his never talking went, she couldn't find any fault with that; Mr. Worthington was just as bad, if he wasn't worse. But Belle's not like me; I don't believe she'd let poor Mr. Worthington talk in the house if he wanted to."

She gradually drifted away from her starting point, and like most people who have usually little to say, became very voluble, when once she passed into the humor of talking. Thérèse let her talk unchecked. It seemed to do her good to chatter about Belle and Lou, and Jack Dawson, and about her home life, of which she unknowingly made such a pitiable picture to her listener.

"I guess David never let on to you about himself," she said moodily, having come back to the sore that rankled: the dread that Thérèse had laid all the blame of the rupture on her shoulders.

"You're mistaken, Mrs. Hosmer. It was a knowledge of his own short-comings that prompted your husband to go back and ask your forgiveness. You must grant, there's nothing in his conduct now that you could reproach him with. And," she added, laying her hand gently on Fanny's arm, "I know you'll be strong, and do your share in this reconciliation—do what you can to please him."

Fanny flushed uneasily under Thérèse's appealing glance.

"I'm willing to do anything that David wants," she replied, "I made up my mind to that from the start. He's a mighty good husband now, Mrs. Laferm. Don't mind what I said about him. I was afraid you thought that—"

"Never mind," returned Thérèse kindly, "I know all about it. Don't worry any farther over what I may think. I believe in you and in him, and I know you'll both be brave and do what's right."

"There isn't anything so very hard for David to do," she said, depressed with a sense of her inadequate strength to do the task which she had set herself. "He's got no faults to give up. David never did have any faults. He's a true, honest man; and I was a coward to say those things about him."

Melicent and Grégoire were coming across the lawn to join the two, and Fanny, seeing them approach, suddenly chilled and wrapt herself about in her mantle of reserve.

"I guess I better go," she said, offering to rise, but Thérèse held out a detaining hand.

"You don't want to go and sit alone in the cottage; stay here with me till Mr. Hosmer comes back from the mill."

Grégoire's face was a study. Melicent, who did what she wanted with him, had chosen this afternoon, for some inscrutable reason, to make him happy. He carried her shawl and parasol; she herself bearing a veritable armful of flowers, leaves, red berried sprigs, a tangle of richest color. They had been in the woods and she had bedecked him with garlands and festoons of autumn leaves, till he looked a very Satyr; a character which his flushed, swarthy cheeks, and glittering animal eyes did not belie.

They were laughing immoderately, and their whole bearing still reflected their exuberant gaiety as they joined Thérèse and Fanny.

"What a 'Mater Dolorosa' Fanny looks!" exclaimed Melicent, throwing herself into a picturesque attitude on the bench beside Thérèse, and resting her feet on Hector's broad back.

Fanny offered no reply, but to look helplessly resigned; an expression which Melicent knew of old, and which had always the effect of irritating her. Not now, however, for the curve of the bench around the great cedar tree removed her from the possibility of contemplating Fanny's doleful visage, unless she made an effort to that end, which she was certainly not inclined to do.

"No, Grégoire," she said, flinging a rose into his face when he would have seated himself beside her, "go sit by Fanny and do something to make her laugh; only don't tickle her; David mightn't like it. And here's Mrs. Lafirme looking almost as glum. Now, if David would only join us with that 'pale cast of thought' that he bears about usually, what a merry go round we'd have."

"When Melicent looks at the world laughing, she wants it to laugh back at her," said Thérèse, reflecting something of the girl's gaiety.

"As in a looking-glass, well isn't that square?" she returned, falling into slang, in her recklessness of spirit.

Endeavoring to guard her treasure of flowers from Thérèse, who was without ceremony making a critical selection among them of what pleased her, Melicent slid around the bench, bringing herself close to

Grégoire and begging his protection against the Vandalism of his aunt. She looked into his eyes for an instant as though asking him for love instead of so slight a favor and he grasped her arm, pressing it till she cried out from the pain: which act, on his side, served to drive her again around to Thérèse.

"Guess what we are going to do to-morrow: you and I and all of us; Grégoire and David and Fanny and everybody?"

"Going to Bedlam along with you?" Thérèse asked.

"Mrs. Lafirme is in need of a rebuke, which I shall proceed to administer," thrusting a crumpled handful of rose leaves down the neck of Thérèse's dress, and laughing joyously in her scuffle to accomplish the punishment.

"No, madam; I don't go to Bedlam; I drive others there. Ask Grégoire what we're going to do. Tell them, Grégoire."

"They ain't much to tell. We'a goin' hoss back ridin'."

"Not me; I can't ride," wailed Fanny.

"You can get up Torpedo for Mrs. Hosmer, can't you, Grégoire?" asked Thérèse.

"Certainly. W'y you could ride ole Torpedo, Mrs. Hosma, if you nova saw a hoss in yo' life. A li'l chile could manage him."

Fanny turned to Thérèse for further assurance and found all that she looked for.

"We'll go up on the hill and see that dear old Morico, and I shall take along a comb, and comb out that exquisite white hair of his and then I shall focus him, seated in his low chair and making one of those cute turkey fans."

"Ole Morico ain't goin' to let you try no monkeyshines on him; I tell you that befo' han'," said Grégoire, rising and coming to Melicent to rid him of his sylvan ornamentations, for it was time for him to leave them. When he turned away, Melicent rose and flung all her flowery wealth into Thérèse's lap, and following took his arm.

"Where are you going?" asked Thérèse.

"Going to help Grégoire feed the mules," she called back looking over her shoulder; the sinking sun lighting her handsome mischievous face.

Thérèse proceeded to arrange the flowers with some regard to graceful symmetry; and Fanny did not regain her talkative spirit that Melicent's coming had put to flight, but sat looking silent and listlessly into the distance.

As Thérèse glanced casually up into her face she saw it warmed by a sudden faint glow—an unusual animation, and following her gaze, she saw that Hosmer had returned and was entering the cottage.

"I guess I better be going," said Fanny rising, and this time Thérèse no longer detained her.

IV

Thérèse Crosses the River

To shirk any serious duties of life would have been entirely foreign to Thérèse's methods or even instincts. But there did come to her moments of rebellion—or repulsion, against the small demands that presented themselves with an unfailing recurrence; and from such, she at times indulged herself with the privilege of running away. When Fanny left her alone—a pathetic little droop took possession of the corners of her mouth that might not have come there if she had not been alone. She laid the flowers, only half arranged, on the bench beside her, as a child would put aside a toy that no longer interested it. She looked towards the house and could see the servants going back and forth. She knew if she entered, she would be met by appeals from one and the other. The overseer would soon be along, with his crib keys, and stable keys; his account of the day's doings and consultations for to-morrow's work, and for the moment, she would have none of it.

"Come, Hector—come, old boy," she said rising abruptly; and crossing the lawn she soon gained the gravel path that led to the outer road. This road brought her by a mild descent to the river bank. The water, seldom stationary for any long period, was at present running low and sluggishly between its red banks.

Tied to the landing was a huge flat-boat, that was managed by the aid of a stout cable reaching quite across the river; and beside it nestled a small light skiff. In this Thérèse seated herself, and proceeded to row across the stream, Hector plunging into the water and swimming in advance of her.

The banks on the opposite shore were almost perpendicular; and their summit to be reached only by the artificial road that had been cut into them: broad and of easy ascent. This river front was a standing worry to Thérèse, for when the water was high and rapid, the banks caved constantly, carrying away great sections from the land. Almost every year, the fences in places had to be moved back, not only for security, but to allow a margin for the road that on this side followed the course of the small river.

High up and perilously near the edge, stood a small cabin. It had once been far removed from the river, which had now, however, eaten its way close up to it—leaving no space for the road-way. The house was somewhat more pretentious than others of its class, being fashioned of planed painted boards, and having a brick chimney that stood fully exposed at one end. A great rose tree climbed and spread generously over one side, and the big red roses grew by hundreds amid the dark green setting of their leaves.

At the gate of this cabin Thérèse stopped, calling out, "*Grosse tante!—oh, Grosse tante!*"

The sound of her voice brought to the door a negress—coal black and so enormously fat that she moved about with evident difficulty. She was dressed in a loosely hanging purple calico garment of the mother Hubbard type—known as a *volante* amongst Louisiana Creoles; and on her head was knotted and fantastically twisted a bright *tignon*. Her glistening good-natured countenance illuminated at the sight of Thérèse.

"*Quo faire to pas woulez rentrer, Tite maîtresse?*" and Thérèse answered in the same Creole dialect: "Not now, *Grosse tante*—I shall be back in half an hour to drink a cup of coffee with you." No English words can convey the soft music of that speech, seemingly made for tenderness and endearment.

As Thérèse turned away from the gate, the black woman re-entered the house, and as briskly as her cumbersome size would permit, began preparations for her mistress' visit. Milk and butter were taken from the safe; eggs, from the India rush basket that hung against the wall; and flour, from the half barrel that stood in convenient readiness in the corner: for *Tite maîtresse* was to be treated to a dish of *croquignoles*. Coffee was always an accomplished fact at hand in the chimney corner.

Grosse tante, or more properly, Marie Louise, was a Creole—Thérèse's nurse and attendant from infancy, and the only one of the family servants who had come with her mistress from New Orleans to Place-du-Bois at that lady's marriage with Jérôme Lafirme. But her ever increasing weight had long since removed her from the possibility of usefulness, otherwise than in supervising her small farm yard. She had little use for "*ces néges Américains,*" as she called the plantation hands—a restless lot forever shifting about and changing quarters.

It was seldom now that she crossed the river; only two occasions being considered of sufficient importance to induce her to such effort. One was in the event of her mistress' illness, when she would install herself at her bedside as a fixture, not to be dislodged by any less inducement than Thérèse's full recovery. The other was when a dinner of importance was to be given: then Marie Louise consented to act as *chef de cuisine*, for there was no more famous cook than she in the State; her instructor having been no less a personage than old Lucien Santien—a *gourmet* famed for his ultra Parisian tastes.

Seated at the base of a great China-berry on whose gnarled protruding roots she rested an arm languidly, Thérèse looked out over the river and gave herself up to doubts and misgivings. She first took exception with herself for that constant interference in the concerns of other people. Might not this propensity be carried too far at times? Did the good accruing counterbalance the personal discomfort into which she was often driven by her own agency? What reason had she to know that a policy of non-interference in the affairs of others might not after all be the judicious one? As much as she tried to vaguely generalize, she found her reasoning applying itself to her relation with Hosmer.

The look which she had surprised in Fanny's face had been a painful revelation to her. Yet could she have expected other, and should she have hoped for less, than that Fanny should love her husband and he in turn should come to love his wife?

Had she married Hosmer herself! Here she smiled to think of the storm of indignation that such a marriage would have roused in the parish. Yet, even facing the impossibility of such contingency, it pleased her to indulge in a short dream of what might have been.

If it were her right instead of another's to watch for his coming and rejoice at it! Hers to call him husband and lavish on him the love that awoke so strongly when she permitted herself, as she was doing now, to invoke it! She felt what capability lay within her of rousing the man to new interests in life. She pictured the dawn of an unsuspected happiness coming to him: broadening; illuminating; growing in him to answer to her own big-heartedness.

Were Fanny, and her own prejudices, worth the sacrifice which she and Hosmer had made? This was the doubt that bade fair to unsettle her; that called for a sharp, strong out-putting of the will before she could bring herself to face the situation without its accessions of personalities. Such communing with herself could not be condemned as a weakness with Thérèse, for the effect which it left upon her strong nature was one of added courage and determination.

When she reached Marie Louise's cabin again, twilight, which is so brief in the South, was giving place to the night.

Within the cabin, the lamp had already been lighted, and Marie Louise was growing restless at Thérèse's long delay.

"Ah *Grosse tante*, I'm so tired," she said, falling into a chair near the door; not relishing the warmth of the room after her quick walk, and wishing to delay as long as possible the necessity of sitting at table. At another time she might have found the dish of golden brown *croquignoles* very tempting with its accessory of fragrant coffee; but not to-day.

"Why do you run about so much, *Tite maîtresse*? You are always going this way and that way; on horseback, on foot—through the house. Make those lazy niggers work more. You spoil them. I tell you if it was old mistress that had to deal with them, they would see something different."

She had taken all the pins from Thérèse's hair which fell in a gleaming, heavy mass; and with her big soft hands she was stroking her head as gently as if those hands had been of the whitest and most delicate.

"I know that look in your eyes, it means headache. It's time for me to make you some more *eau sédative*—I am sure you haven't any more; you've given it away as you give away every thing."

"*Grosse tante*," said Thérèse seated at table and sipping her coffee; *Grosse tante* also drinking her cup—but seated apart, "I am going to insist on having your cabin moved back; it is silly to be so stubborn about such a small matter. Some day you will find yourself out in the middle of the river—and what am I going to do then?—no one to nurse me when I am sick—no one to scold me—nobody to love me."

"Don't say that, *Tite maîtresse*, all the world loves you—it isn't only Marie Louise. But no. You must remember the last time poor Monsieur Jérôme moved me, and said with a laugh that I can never forget, 'well, *Grosse tante*, I know we have got you far enough this time out of danger,' away back in Dumont's field you recollect? I said then, Marie Louise will move no more; she's too old. If the good God does not want to take care of me, then it's time for me to go."

"Ah but, *Grosse tante*, remember—God does not want all the trouble on his own shoulders," Thérèse answered humoring the woman, in her conception of the Deity. "He wants us to do our share, too."

"Well, I have done my share. Nothing is going to harm Marie Louise. I thought about all that, do not fret. So the last time Père Antoine passed in the road—going down to see that poor Pierre Pardou at the Mouth—I called him in, and he blessed the whole house inside and out, with holy water—notice how the roses have bloomed since then—and gave me medals of the holy Virgin to hang about. Look over the door, *Tite maîtresse*, how it shines, like a silver star."

"If you will not have your cabin removed, *Grosse tante*, then come live with me. Old Hatton has wanted work at Place-du-Bois, the longest time. We will have him build you a room wherever you choose, a pretty little house like those in the city."

"*Non—non, Tite maîtresse, Marie Louise 'prè créver icite avé tous son butin, si faut*" (no, no, *Tite maîtresse*, Marie Louise will die here with all her belongings if it must be).

The servants were instructed that when their mistress was not at home at a given hour, her absence should cause no delay in the household arrangements. She did not choose that her humor or her movements be hampered by a necessity of regularity which she owed to no one. When she reached home supper had long been over.

Nearing the house she heard the scraping of Nathan's violin, the noise of shuffling feet and unconstrained laughter. These festive sounds came from the back veranda. She entered the dining-room, and from its obscurity looked out on a curious scene. The veranda was lighted by a lamp suspended from one of its pillars. In a corner sat Nathan; serious, dignified, scraping out a monotonous but rhythmic minor strain to which two young negroes from the lower quarters—famous dancers—were keeping time in marvelous shuffling and pigeon-wings; twisting their supple joints into astonishing contortions and the sweat rolling from their black visages. A crowd of darkies stood at a respectful distance an appreciative and encouraging audience. And seated on the broad rail of the veranda were Melicent and Grégoire, patting Juba and singing a loud accompaniment to the breakdown.

Was this the Grégoire who had only yesterday wept such bitter tears on his aunt's bosom?

Thérèse turning away from the scene, the doubt assailed her whether it were after all worth while to strive against the sorrows of life that can be so readily put aside.

V

One Afternoon

Whatever may have been Torpedo's characteristics in days gone by, at this advanced period in his history he possessed none so striking as a stoical inaptitude for being moved. Another of his distinguishing traits was a propensity for grazing which he was prone to indulge at inopportune moments. Such points taken in conjunction with a gait closely resembling that of the camel in the desert, might give much cause to wonder at Thérèse's motive in recommending him as a suitable mount for the unfortunate Fanny, were it not for his widespread reputation of angelic inoffensiveness.

The ride which Melicent had arranged and in which she held out such promises of a "lark" proved after all but a desultory affair. For with Fanny making but a sorry equestrian debut and Hosmer creeping along at her side; Thérèse unable to hold Beauregard within conventional limits, and Melicent and Grégoire vanishing utterly from the scene, sociability was a feature entirely lacking to the excursion.

"David, I can't go another step: I just can't, so that settles it."

The look of unhappiness in Fanny's face and attitude, would have moved the proverbial stone.

"I think if you change horses with me, Fanny, you'll find it more comfortable, and we'll turn about and go home."

"I wouldn't get on that horse's back, David Hosmer, if I had to die right here in the woods, I wouldn't."

"Do you think you could manage to walk back that distance then? I can lead the horses," he suggested as a *pis aller*.

"I guess I'll haf to; but goodness knows if I'll ever get there alive."

They were far up on the hill, which spot they had reached by painfully slow and labored stages, each refraining from mention of a discomfort that might interfere with the supposed enjoyment of the other, till Fanny's note of protest.

Hosmer cast about him for some expedient that might lighten the unpleasantness of the situation, when a happy thought occurred to him.

"If you'll try to bear up, a few yards further, you can dismount at old Morico's cabin and I'll hurry back and get the buggy. It can be driven this far anyway: and it's only a short walk from here through the woods."

So Hosmer set her down before Morico's door: her long riding skirt, borrowed for the occasion, twisting awkwardly around her legs, and every joint in her body aching.

Partly by pantomimic signs interwoven with a few French words which he had picked up within the last year, Hosmer succeeded in making himself understood to the old man, and rode away leaving Fanny in his care.

Morico fussily preceded her into the house and placed a great clumsy home-made rocker at her disposal, into which she cast herself with every appearance of bodily distress. He then busied himself in tidying up the room out of deference to his guest; gathering up the scissors, waxen thread and turkey feathers which had fallen from his lap in his disturbance, and laying them on the table. He knocked the ashes from his corn-cob pipe which he now rested on a projection of the brick chimney that extended into the room and that served as mantelpiece. All the while he cast snatched glances at Fanny, who sat pale and tired. Her appearance seemed to move him to make an effort towards relieving it. He took a key from his pocket and unlocking a side of the *garde manger*, drew forth a small flask of whisky. Fanny had closed her eyes and was not aware of his action, till she heard him at her elbow saying in his feeble quavering voice:—

"*Tenez madame; goutez un peu: ça va vous faire du bien,*" and opening her eyes she saw that he held a glass half filled with strong "toddy" for her acceptance.

She thrust out her hand to ward it away as though it had been a reptile that menaced her with its sting.

Morico looked nonplussed and a little abashed: but he had much faith in the healing qualities of his remedy and urged it on her anew. She trembled a little, and looked away with rather excited eyes.

"*Je vous assure madame, ça ne peut pas vous faire du mal.*"

Fanny took the glass from his hand, and rising went and placed it on the table, then walked to the open door and looked eagerly out, as though hoping for the impossibility of her husband's return.

She did not seat herself again, but walked restlessly about the room, intently examining its meager details. The circuit of inspection bringing her again to the table, she picked up Morico's turkey fan, looking at it long and critically. When she laid it down, it was to seize the glass of "toddy" which she unhesitatingly put to her lips and drained at a draught. All uneasiness and fatigue seemed to leave her on the instant as though by magic. She went back to her chair and reseated herself composedly. Her eyes now rested on her old host with a certain quizzical curiosity strange to them.

He was plainly demoralized by her presence, and still made pretense of occupying himself with the arrangement of the room.

Presently she said to him: "Your remedy did me more good than I'd expected," but not understanding her, he only smiled and looked at her blankly.

She laughed good-humoredly back at him, then went to the table and poured from the flask which he had left standing there, liquor to the depth of two fingers, this time drinking it more deliberately. After that she tried to talk to Morico and thought it very amusing that he could not understand her.

Presently Joçint came home and accepted her presence there very indifferently. He went to the *garde manger* to stay his hunger, much as he had done on the occasion of Thérèse's visit; talked in grum abrupt utterances to his father, and disappeared into the adjoining room where Fanny could hear him and occasionally see him polishing and oiling his cherished rifle.

Morico, more accustomed to foreign sounds in the woods than she, was the first to detect the approach of Grégoire, whom he went out hurriedly to meet, glad of the relief from the supposed necessity of entertaining his puzzling visitor. When he was fairly out of the room, she arose quickly, approached the table and reaching for the flask of liquor, thrust it hastily into her pocket, then went to join him. At the moment that Grégoire came up, Joçint issued from a side door and stood looking at the group.

"Well, Mrs. Hosma, yere I am. I reckon you was tired waitin'. The buggy's yonda in the road."

He shook hands cordially with Morico saying something to him in French which made the old man laugh heartily.

"Why didn't David come? I thought he said he was coming; that's the way he does," said Fanny complainingly.

"That's a po' compliment to me, Mrs. Hosrma. Can't you stan' my company for that li'le distance?" returned Grégoire gallantly. "Mr. Hosma had a good deal to do w'en he got back, that's w'y he sent me. An' we betta hurry up if we expec' to git any suppa' to-night. Like as not you'll fine your kitchen cleaned out."

Fanny looked her inquiry for his meaning.

"Why, don't you know this is 'Tous-saint' eve—w'en the dead git out o' their graves an' walk about? You wouldn't ketch a nigga out o' his cabin to-night afta dark to save his soul. They all gittin' ready now to hustle back to the quartas."

"That's nonsense," said Fanny, drawing on her gloves, "you ought to have more sense than to repeat such things."

Grégoire laughed, looking surprised at her unusual energy of speech and manner. Then he turned to Joçint, whose presence he had thus far ignored, and asked in a peremptory tone:

"W'at did Woodson say 'bout watchin' at the mill to-night? Did you ask him like I tole you?"

"Yaas, me ax um: ee' low ee an' goin'. Say how Sylveste d'wan' watch lak alluz. Say ee an' goin'. Me don' blem 'im neida, don' ketch me out de 'ouse night lak dat fu no man."

"*Sacré imbécile*," muttered Grégoire, between his teeth, and vouchsafed him no other answer, but nodded to Morico and turned away. Fanny followed with a freedom of movement quite unlike that of her coming.

Morico went into the house and coming back hastily to the door called to Joçint:

"Bring back that flask of whisky that you took off the table."

"You're a liar: you know I have no use for whisky. That's one of your damned tricks to make me buy you more." And he seated himself on an over-turned tub and with his small black eyes half closed, looked moodily out into the solemn darkening woods. The old man showed no resentment at the harshness and disrespect of his son's speech, being evidently used to such. He passed his hand slowly over his white long hair and turned bewildered into the house.

"Is it just this same old thing year in and year out, Grégoire? Don't any one ever get up a dance, or a card party or anything?"

"Jus' as you say; the same old thing f'om one yea's en' to the otha. I used to think it was putty lonesome myse'f w'en I firs' come yere. Then you see they's no neighbo's right roun' yere. In Natchitoches now; that's the place to have a right down good time. But see yere; I didn' know you was fon' o' dancin' an' such things."

"Why, of course, I just dearly love to dance. But it's as much as my life's worth to say that before David; he's such a stick; but I guess you know that by this time," with a laugh, as he had never heard from her before—so unconstrained; at the same time drawing nearer to him and looking merrily into his face.

"The little lady's been having a 'toddy' at Morico's, that makes her lively," thought Grégoire. But the knowledge did not abash him in the least. He accommodated himself at once to the situation with that adaptability common to the American youth, whether of the South, North, East or West.

"Where abouts did you leave David when you come away?" she asked with a studied indifference.

"Hol' on there, Buckskin—w'ere you takin' us? W'y, I lef' him at the sto' mailin' lettas."

"Had the others all got back? Mrs. Laferm? Melicent? did they all stop at the store, too?"

"Who? Aunt Thrérèse? no, she was up at the house w'en I lef'—I reckon Miss Melicent was there too. Talkin' 'bout fun,—it's to git into one o' them big spring wagons on a moonlight night, like they do in Centaville sometimes; jus' packed down with young folks—and start out fur a dance up the coast. They ain't nothin' to beat it as fah as fun goes."

"It must be just jolly. I guess you're a pretty good dancer, Grégoire?"

"Well—'taint fur me to say. But they ain't many can out dance me: not in Natchitoches pa'ish, anyway. I can say that much."

If such a thing could have been, Fanny would have startled Grégoire more than once during the drive home. Before its close she had obtained a promise from him to take her up to Natchitoches for the very next entertainment,—averring that she didn't care what David said. If he wanted to bury himself that was his own look out. And if Mrs. Laferm took people to be angels that they could live in a place like that, and give up everything and not have any kind of enjoyment out of life, why, she was mistaken and that's all there was to it. To all of which freely expressed views Grégoire emphatically assented.

Hosmer had very soon disembarrassed himself of Torpedo, knowing that the animal would unerringly find his way to the corn crib by supper time. He continued his own way now untrammelled, and at an agreeable speed which soon brought him to the spring at the road side. Here he found Thérèse, half seated against a projection of rock, in her hand a bunch of ferns which she had evidently dismounted to gather, and holding Beauregard's bridle while he munched at the cool wet tufts of grass that grew everywhere.

As Hosmer rode up at a rapid pace, he swung himself from his horse almost before the animal came to a full stop. He removed his hat, mopped his forehead, stamped about a little to relax his limbs and turned to answer the enquiry with which Thérèse met him.

"Left her at Morico's. I'll have to send the buggy back for her."

"I can't forgive myself for such a blunder," said Thérèse regretfully, "indeed I had no idea of that miserable beast's character. I never was on him you know—only the little darkies, and they never complained: they'd as well ride cows as not."

"Oh, it's mainly from her being unaccustomed to riding, I believe."

This was the first time that Hosmer and Thérèse had met alone since his return from St. Louis. They looked at each other with full consciousness of what lay in the other's mind. Thérèse felt that however adroitly another woman might have managed the situation, for herself, it would have been a piece of affectation to completely ignore it at this moment.

"Mr. Hosmer, perhaps I ought to have said something before this, to you—about what you've done."

"Oh, yes, congratulated me—complimented me," he replied with a pretense at a laugh.

"Well, the latter, perhaps. I think we all like to have our good and right actions recognized for their worth."

He flushed, looked at her with a smile, then laughed out-right—this time it was no pretense.

"So I've been a good boy; have done as my mistress bade me and now I'm to receive a condescending little pat on the head—and of course must say thank you. Do you know, Mrs. Lafirme—and I don't see why a woman like you oughtn't to know it—it's one of those things to drive a man mad, the sweet complaisance with which women accept situations, or inflict situations that it takes the utmost of a man's strength to endure."

"Well, Mr. Hosmer," said Thérèse plainly discomposed, "you must concede you decided it was the right thing to do."

"I didn't do it because I thought it was right, but because you thought it was right. But that makes no difference."

"Then remember your wife is going to do the right thing herself—she admitted as much to me."

"Don't you fool yourself, as Melicent says, about what Mrs. Hosmer means to do. I take no account of it. But you take it so easily; so as a matter of course. That's what exasperates me. That you, you, you, shouldn't have a suspicion of the torture of it; the loathsomeness of it. But how could you—how could any woman understand it? Oh forgive me, Thérèse—I wouldn't want you to. There's no brute so brutal as a man," he cried, seeing the pain in her face and knowing he had caused it. "But you know you promised to help me—oh I'm talking like an idiot."

"And I do," returned Thérèse, "that is, I want to, I mean to."

"Then don't tell me again that I have done right. Only look at me sometimes a little differently than you do at Hiram or the gate post. Let me once in a while see a look in your face that tells me that you understand—if it's only a little bit."

Thérèse thought it best to interrupt the situation; so, pale and silently she prepared to mount her horse. He came to her assistance of course, and when she was seated she drew off her loose riding glove and held out her hand to him. He pressed it gratefully, then touched it with his lips; then turned it and kissed the half open palm.

She did not leave him this time, but rode at his side in silence with a frown and little line of thought between her blue eyes.

As they were nearing the store she said diffidently: "Mr. Hosmer, I wonder if it wouldn't be best for you to put the mill in some one else's charge—and go away from Place-du-Bois."

"I believe you always speak with a purpose, Mrs. Lafirme: you have somebody's ultimate good in view, when you say that. Is it your own, or mine or whose is it?"

"Oh! not mine."

"I will leave Place-du-Bois, certainly, if you wish it."

As she looked at him she was forced to admit that she had never seen him look as he did now. His face, usually serious, had a whole unwritten tragedy in it. And she felt altogether sore and puzzled and exasperated over man's problematic nature.

"I don't think it should be left entirely to me to say. Doesn't your own reason suggest a proper course in the matter?"

"My reason is utterly unable to determine anything in which you are concerned. Mrs. Lafirme," he said checking his horse and laying a restraining hand on her bridle, "let me speak to you one moment. I know you are a woman to whom one may speak the truth. Of course, you remember that you prevailed upon me to go back to my wife. To you it seemed the right thing—to me it seemed certainly hard—but no more nor less than taking up the old unhappy routine of life, where

I had left it when I quitted her. I reasoned much like a stupid child who thinks the colors in his kaleidoscope may fall twice into the same design. In place of the old, I found an entirely new situation—horrid, sickening, requiring such a strain upon my energies to live through it, that I believe it's an absurdity to waste so much moral force for so poor an aim—there would be more dignity in putting an end to my life. It doesn't make it any the more bearable to feel that the cause of this unlooked for change lies within myself—my altered feelings. But it seems to me that I have the right to ask you not to take yourself out of my life; your moral support; your bodily atmosphere. I hope not to give way to the weakness of speaking of these things again: but before you leave me, tell me, do you understand a little better why I need you?"

"Yes, I understand now; and I thank you for talking so openly to me. Don't go away from Place-du-Bois: it would make me very wretched."

She said no more and he was glad of it, for her last words held almost the force of action for him; as though she had let him feel for an instant her heart beat against his own with an echoing pain.

Their ways now diverged. She went in the direction of the house and he to the store where he found Grégoire, whom he sent for his wife.

VI

One Night

"Grégoire was right: do you know those nasty creatures have gone and left every speck of the supper dishes unwashed? I've got half a mind to give them both warning to-morrow morning."

Fanny had come in from the kitchen to the sitting-room, and the above homily was addressed to her husband who stood lighting his cigar. He had lately taken to smoking.

"You'd better do nothing of the kind; you wouldn't find it easy to replace them. Put up a little with their vagaries: this sort of thing only happens once a year."

"How do you know it won't be something else just as ridiculous to-morrow? And that idiot of a Minervy; what do you suppose she told me when I insisted on her staying to wash up things? She says, last whatever you call it, her husband wanted to act hard-headed and staid out after dark, and when he was crossing the bayou, the spirits jerked him off his horse and dragged him up and down in the water, till he was nearly drowned. I don't see what you're laughing at; I guess you'd like to make out that they're in the right."

Hosmer was perfectly aware that Fanny had had a drink, and he rightly guessed that Morico had given it to her. But he was at a loss to account for the increasing symptoms of intoxication that she showed. He tried to persuade her to go to bed; but his efforts to that end remained unheeded, till she had eased her mind of an accumulation of grievances, mostly fancied. He had much difficulty in preventing her from going over to give Melicent a piece of her mind about her lofty airs and arrogance in thinking herself better than other people. And she was very eager to tell Thérèse that she meant to do as she liked, and would stand no poking of noses in her business. It was a good while before she fell into a heavy sleep, after shedding a few maudlin tears over the conviction that he intended to leave her again, and clinging to his neck with beseeching enquiry whether he loved her.

He went out on the veranda feeling much as if he had been wrestling with a strong adversary who had mastered him, and whom he was glad to be freed of, even at the cost of coming inglorious from the conflict.

KATE CHOPIN

The night was so dark, so hushed, that if ever the dead had wished to step from their graves and take a stroll above ground, they could not have found a more fitting hour. Hosmer walked very long in the soothing quiet. He would have liked to walk the night through. The last three hours had been like an acute physical pain, that was over for the moment, and that being over, left his mind free to return to the delicious consciousness, that he had needed to be reminded of, that Thérèse loved him after all. When his measured tread upon the veranda finally ceased to mark the passing hours, a quiet that was almost pulseless fell upon the plantation. Place-du-Bois slept. Perhaps the only night in the year that some or other of the negroes did not lurk in fence corners, or make exchange of nocturnal visits.

But out in the hills there was no such unearthly stillness reigning. Those restless wood-dwellers, that never sleep, were sending startling gruesome calls to each other. Bats were flapping and whirling and darting hither and thither; the gliding serpent making quick rustle amid the dry, crisp leaves, and over all sounded the murmur of the great pine trees, telling their mystic secrets to the night.

A human creature was there too, feeling a close fellowship with these spirits of night and darkness; with no more fear in his heart than the unheeded serpent crossing his path. Every inch of the ground he knew. He wanted no daylight to guide him. Had his eyes been blinded he would no doubt have bent his body close to earth and scented his way along like the human hound that he was. Over his shoulder hung the polished rifle that sent dull and sudden gleamings into the dark. A large tin pail swung from his hand. He was very careful of this pail—or its contents, for he feared to lose a drop. And when he accidentally struck an intervening tree and spilled some upon the ground, he muttered a curse against his own awkwardness.

Twice since leaving his cabin up in the clearing, he had turned to drive back his yellow skulking dog that followed him. Each time the brute had fled in abject terror, only to come creeping again into his master's footsteps, when he thought himself forgotten. Here was a companion whom neither Joçint nor his mission required. Exasperated, he seated himself on a fallen tree and whistled softly. The dog, who had been holding back, dashed to his side, trembling with eagerness, and striving to twist his head around to lick the hand that patted him. Joçint's other hand glided quickly into his pocket, from which he drew forth a coil of thin rope that he flung deftly over the animal's head, drawing it close and tight about the homely, shaggy throat. So quickly was the action done, that no sound was uttered, and Joçint continued his way untroubled by his old and faithful friend, whom he left hanging to the limb of a tree.

He was following the same path that he traversed daily to and from the mill, and which soon brought him out into the level with its soft tufted grass and clumps of squat thorn trees. There was no longer the protecting wood to screen him; but of such there was no need, for the darkness hung about him like the magic mantle of story. Nearing the mill he grew cautious, creeping along with the tread of a stealthy beast, and halting at intervals to listen for sounds that he wished not to hear. He knew there was no one on guard tonight. A movement in the bushes near by, made him fall quick and sprawling to earth. It was only Grégoire's horse munching the soft grass. Joçint drew near and laid his hand on the horse's back. It was hot and reeking with sweat. Here was a fact to make him more wary. Horses were not found in such condition from quietly grazing of a cool autumn night. He seated himself upon the ground, with his hands clasped about his knees, all doubled up in a little heap, and waited there with the patience of the savage, letting an hour go by, whilst he made no movement.

The hour past, he stole towards the mill, and began his work of sprinkling the contents of his pail here and there along the dry timbers at well calculated distances, with care that no drop should be lost. Then, he drew together a great heap of crisp shavings and slathers, plentifully besprinkling it with what remained in the can. When he had struck a match against his rough trousers and placed it carefully in the midst of this small pyramid, he found that he had done his work but too surely. The quick flame sprang into life, seizing at once all it could reach. Leaping over intervals; effacing the darkness that had shrouded him; seeming to mock him as a fool and point him out as a target for heaven and earth to hurl destruction at if they would. Where should he hide himself? He only thought now of how he might have done the deed differently, and with safety to himself. He stood with great beams and loose planks surrounding him; quaking with a premonition of evil. He wanted to fly in one direction; then thought it best to follow the opposite; but a force outside of himself seemed to hold him fast to one spot. When turning suddenly about, he knew it was too late, he felt that all was lost, for there was Grégoire, not twenty paces away—covering him with the muzzle of a pistol and—cursed luck—his own rifle along with the empty pail in the raging fire.

Thérèse was passing a restless night. She had lain long awake, dwelling on the insistent thoughts that the day's happenings had given rise to. The sleep which finally came to her was troubled by dreams—demoniac—grotesque. Hosmer was in a danger from which she was striving with physical effort to rescue him, and when she dragged him painfully from the peril that menaced him, she turned to see that it was Fanny whom she had saved—laughing at her derisively, and Hosmer had been left to perish. The dream was agonizing; like an appalling nightmare. She awoke in a fever of distress, and raised herself in bed to shake off the unnatural impression which such a dream can leave. The curtains were drawn aside from the window that faced her bed, and looking out she saw a long tongue of flame, reaching far up into the sky—away over the tree tops and the whole Southern horizon a glow. She knew at once that the mill was burning, and it was the affair of a moment with her to spring from her bed and don slippers and wrapper. She knocked on Melicent's door to acquaint her with the startling news; then hurried out into the back yard and rang the plantation bell.

Next she was at the cottage rousing Hosmer. But the alarm of the bell had already awakened him, and he was dressed and out on the porch almost as soon as Thérèse had called. Melicent joined them, highly agitated, and prepared to contribute her share towards any scene that might be going forward. But she found little encouragement for heroics with Hosmer. In saddling his horse rather hastily he was as unmoved as though preparing for an uneventful morning canter. He stood at the foot of the stairs preparing to mount when Grégoire rode up as if pursued by furies; checking his horse with a quick, violent wrench that set it quivering in its taut limbs.

"Well," said Hosmer, "I guess it's done for. How did it happen? who did it?"

"Joçint's work," answered Grégoire bitingly.

"The damned scoundrel," muttered Hosmer, "where is he?"

"Don' botha 'bout Joçint; he ain't goin' to set no mo' mill afire," saying which, he turned his horse and the two rode furiously away.

Melicent grasped Thérèse's arm convulsively.

"What does he mean?" she asked in a frightened whisper.

"I—I don't know," Thérèse faltered. She had clasped her hands spasmodically together, at Grégoire's words, trembling with horror of what must be their meaning.

"May be he arrested him," suggested the girl.

"I hope so. Come; let's go to bed: there's no use staying out here in the cold and dark."

Hosmer had left the sitting-room door open, and Thérèse entered. She approached Fanny's door and knocked twice: not brusquely, but sufficiently loud to be heard from within, by any one who was awake. No answer came, and she went away, knowing that Fanny slept.

The unusual sound of the bell, ringing two hours past midnight—that very deadest hour of the night—had roused the whole plantation. On all sides squads of men and a few venturesome women were hurrying towards the fire; the dread of supernatural encounters overcome for the moment by such strong reality and by the confidence lent them in each other's company.

There were many already gathered around the mill, when Grégoire and Hosmer reached it. All effort to save anything had been abandoned as useless. The books and valuables had been removed from the office. The few householders—mill-hands—whose homes were close by, had carried their scant belongings to places of safety, but everything else was given over to the devouring flames.

The heat from this big raging fire was intense, and had driven most of the gaping spectators gradually back—almost into the woods. But there, to one side, where the fire was rapidly gaining, and making itself already uncomfortably felt, stood a small awe-stricken group talking in whispers; their ignorance and superstition making them irresolute to lay a hand upon the dead Joçint. His body lay amongst the heavy timbers, across a huge beam, with arms outstretched and head hanging down upon the ground. The glazed eyes were staring up into the red sky, and on his swarthy visage was yet the horror which had come there, when he looked in the face of death.

"In God's name, what are you doing?" cried Hosmer. "Can't some of you carry that boy's body to a place of safety?"

Grégoire had followed, and was looking down indifferently at the dead. "Come, len' a han' there; this is gittin' too durn hot," he said, stooping to raise the lifeless form. Hosmer was preparing to help him. But there was some one staggering through the crowd; pushing men to right and left. With now a hand upon the breast of both Hosmer and Grégoire, and thrusting them with such force and violence, as to lay them prone amongst the timbers. It was the father. It was old Morico. He had awakened in the night and missed his boy. He had seen the fire; indeed close enough that he could hear its roaring; and he knew everything. The whole story was plain to him as if it had been told by a revealing angel. The strength of his youth had come back to speed him over the ground.

"Murderers!" he cried looking about him with hate in his face. He did not know who had done it; no one knew yet, and he saw in every man he looked upon the possible slayer of his child.

So here he stood over the prostrate figure; his old gray jeans hanging loosely about him; wild eyed—with bare head clasped between his claw-like hands, which the white disheveled hair swept over. Hosmer approached again, offering gently to help him carry his son away.

"Stand back," he hurled at him. But he had understood the offer. His boy must not be left to burn like a log of wood. He bent down and strove to lift the heavy body, but the effort was beyond his strength. Seeing this he stooped again and this time grasped it beneath the arms; then slowly, draggingly, with halting step, began to move backward.

The fire claimed no more attention. All eyes were fastened upon this weird picture; a sight which moved the most callous to offer again and again assistance, that was each time spurned with an added defiance.

Hosmer stood looking on, with folded arms; moved by the grandeur and majesty of the scene. The devouring element, loosed in its awful recklessness there in the heart of this lonely forest. The motley group of black and white standing out in the great red light, powerless to do more than wait and watch. But more was he stirred to the depths of his being, by the sight of this human tragedy enacted before his eyes.

Once, the old man stops in his backward journey. Will he give over? has his strength deserted him? is the thought that seizes every on-looker. But no—with renewed effort he begins again his slow retreat, till at last a sigh of relief comes from the whole watching multitude. Morico with his burden has reached a spot of safety. What will he do next? They watch in breathless suspense. But Morico does nothing. He only stands immovable as a carved image. Suddenly there is a cry that reaches far above the roar of fire and crash of falling timbers: "*Mon fils! mon garçon!*" and the old man totters and falls backward to earth, still clinging to the lifeless body of his son. All hasten towards him. Hosmer reaches him first. And when he gently lifts the dead Joçint, the father this time makes no hinderance, for he too has gone beyond the knowledge of all earthly happenings.

VII

Melicent Leaves Place-du-Bois

There had been no witness to the killing of Joçint; but there were few who did not recognize Grégoire's hand in the affair. When met with the accusation, he denied it, or acknowledged it, or evaded the charge with a jest, as he felt for the moment inclined. It was a deed characteristic of any one of the Santien boys, and if not altogether laudable—Joçint having been at the time of the shooting unarmed—yet was it thought in a measure justified by the heinousness of his offense, and beyond dispute, a benefit to the community.

Hosmer reserved the expression of his opinion. The occurrence once over, with the emotions which it had awakened, he was inclined to look at it from one of those philosophic stand-points of his friend Homeyer. Heredity and pathology had to be considered in relation with the slayer's character. He saw in it one of those interesting problems of human existence that are ever turning up for man's contemplation, but hardly for the exercise of man's individual judgment. He was conscious of an inward repulsion which this action of Grégoire's awakened in him,—much the same as a feeling of disgust for an animal whose instinct drives it to the doing of violent deeds,—yet he made no difference in his manner towards him.

Thérèse was deeply distressed over this double tragedy: feeling keenly the unhappy ending of old Morico. But her chief sorrow came from the callousness of Grégoire, whom she could not move even to an avowal of regret. He could not understand that he should receive any thing but praise for having rid the community of so offensive and dangerous a personage as Joçint; and seemed utterly blind to the moral aspect of his deed.

An event at once so exciting and dramatic as this conflagration, with the attendant deaths of Morico and his son, was much discussed amongst the negroes. They were a good deal of one opinion in regard to Joçint having been only properly served in getting "w'at he done ben lookin' fu' dis long time." Grégoire was rather looked upon as a clever instrument in the Lord's service; and the occurrence pointed a moral which they were not likely to forget.

The burning of the mill entailed much work upon Hosmer, to which he turned with a zest—an absorption that for the time excluded everything else.

Melicent had shunned Grégoire since the shooting. She had avoided speaking with him—even looking at him. During the turmoil which closely followed upon the tragic event, this change in the girl had escaped his notice. On the next day he suspected it only. But the third day brought him the terrible conviction. He did not know that she was making preparations to leave for St. Louis, and quite accidentally overheard Hosmer giving an order to one of the unemployed mill hands to call for her baggage on the following morning before train time.

As much as he had expected her departure, and looked painfully forward to it, this certainty—that she was leaving on the morrow and without a word to him—bewildered him. He abandoned at once the work that was occupying him.

"I didn' know Miss Melicent was goin' away to-morrow," he said in a strange pleading voice to Hosmer.

"Why, yes," Hosmer answered, "I thought you knew. She's been talking about it for a couple of days."

"No, I didn' know nothin' 'tall 'bout it," he said, turning away and reaching for his hat, but with such nerveless hand that he almost dropped it before placing it on his head.

"If you're going to the house," Hosmer called after him, "tell Melicent that Woodson won't go for her trunks before morning. She thought she'd need to have them ready to-night."

"Yes, if I go to the house. I don' know if I'm goin' to the house or not," he replied, walking listlessly away.

Hosmer looked after the young man, and thought of him for a moment: of his soft voice and gentle manner—perplexed that he should be the same who had expressed in confidence the single regret that he had not been able to kill Joçint more than once.

Grégoire went directly to the house, and approached that end of the veranda on which Melicent's room opened. A trunk had already been packed and fastened and stood outside, just beneath the low-silled window that was open. Within the room, and also beneath the window, was another trunk, before which Melicent knelt, filling it more or less systematically from an abundance of woman's toggery that lay in a cumbrous heap on the floor beside her. Grégoire stopped at the window to tell her, with a sad attempt at indifference:

"Yo' brotha says don't hurry packin'; Woodson ain't goin' to come fur your trunks tell mornin'."

"All right, thank you," glancing towards him for an instant carelessly and going on with her work.

"I didn' know you was goin' away."

"That's absurd: you knew all along I was going away," she returned, with countenance as expressionless as feminine subtlety could make it.

"W'y don't you let somebody else do that? Can't you come out yere a w'ile?"

"No, I prefer doing it myself; and I don't care to go out."

What could he do? what could he say? There were no convenient depths in his mind from which he might draw at will, apt and telling speeches to taunt her with. His heart was swelling and choking him, at sight of the eyes that looked anywhere, but in his own; at sight of the lips that he had one time kissed, pressed into an icy silence. She went on with her task of packing, unmoved. He stood a while longer, silently watching her, his hat in his hands that were clasped behind him, and a stupor of grief holding him vise-like. Then he walked away. He felt somewhat as he remembered to have felt oftentimes as a boy, when ill and suffering, his mother would put him to bed and send him a cup of bouillon perhaps, and a little negro to sit beside him. It seemed very cruel to him now that some one should not do something for him— that he should be left to suffer this way. He walked across the lawn over to the cottage, where he saw Fanny pacing slowly up and down the porch.

She saw him approach and stood in a patch of sunlight to wait for him. He really had nothing to say to her as he stood grasping two of the balustrades and looking up at her. He wanted somebody to talk to him about Melicent.

"Did you know Miss Melicent was goin' away?"

Had it been Hosmer or Thérèse asking her the question she would have replied simply "yes," but to Grégoire she said "yes; thank Goodness," as frankly as though she had been speaking to Belle Worthington. "I don't see what's kept her down here all this time, anyway."

"You don't like her?" he asked, stupefied at the strange possibility of any one not loving Melicent to distraction.

"No. You wouldn't either, if you knew her as well as I do. If she likes a person she goes on like a lunatic over them as long as it lasts; then goodbye John! she'll throw them aside as she would an old dress."

"Oh, I believe she thinks a heap of Aunt Thérèse."

"All right; you'll see how much she thinks of Aunt Thérèse. And the people she's been engaged to! There ain't a worse flirt in the city of St. Louis; and always some excuse or other to break it off at the last minute. I haven't got any use for her, Lord knows. There ain't much love lost between us."

"Well, I reckon she knows they ain't anybody born, good enough fur her?" he said, thinking of those engagements that she had shattered.

"What was David doing?" Fanny asked abruptly.

"Writin' lettas at the sto'."

"Did he say when he was coming?"

"No."

"Do you guess he'll come pretty soon?"

"No, I reckon not fur a good w'ile."

"Is Melicent with Mrs. Laferm?"

"No; she's packin' her things."

"I guess I'll go sit with Mrs. Laferm, d'you think she'll mind?"

"No, she'll be glad to have you."

Fanny crossed over to go join Thérèse. She liked to be with her when there was no danger of interruption from Melicent, and Grégoire went wandering aimlessly about the plantation.

He staked great hopes on what the night might bring for him. She would melt, perhaps, to the extent of a smile or one of her old glances. He was almost cheerful when he seated himself at table; only he and his aunt and Melicent. He had never seen her look so handsome as now, in a woolen gown that she had not worn before, of warm rich tint, that brought out a certain regal splendor that he had not suspected in her. A something that she seemed to have held in reserve till this final moment. But she had nothing for him—nothing. All her conversation was addressed to Thérèse; and she hurried away from table at the close of the meal, under pretext of completing her arrangements for departure.

"Doesn't she mean to speak to me?" he asked fiercely of Thérèse.

"Oh, Grégoire, I see so much trouble around me; so many sad mistakes, and I feel so powerless to right them; as if my hands were tied. I can't help you in this; not now. But let me help you in other ways. Will you listen to me?"

"If you want to help me, Aunt," he said stabbing his fork into a piece of bread before him, "go and ask her if she doesn't mean to talk to me: if she won't come out on the gallery a minute."

"Grégoire wants to know if you won't go out and speak to him a moment, Melicent," said Thérèse entering the girl's room. "Do as you wish, of course. But remember you are going away to-morrow; you'll likely never see him again. A friendly word from you now, may do more good than you imagine. I believe he's as unhappy at this moment as a creature can be!"

Melicent looked at her horrified. "I don't understand you at all, Mrs. Lafirme. Think what he's done; murdered a defenseless man! How can you have him near you—seated at your table? I don't know what nerves you have in your bodies, you and David. There's David, hobnobbing with him. Even that Fanny talking to him as if he were blameless. Never! If he were dying I wouldn't go near him."

"Haven't you a spark of humanity in you?" asked Thérèse, flushing violently.

"Oh, this is something physical," she replied, shivering, "let me alone."

Thérèse went out to Grégoire, who stood waiting on the veranda. She only took his hand and pressed it telling him good-night, and he knew that it was a dismissal.

There may be lovers, who, under the circumstances, would have felt sufficient pride to refrain from going to the depôt on the following morning, but Grégoire was not one of them. He was there. He who only a week before had thought that nothing but her constant presence could reconcile him with life, had narrowed down the conditions for his life's happiness now to a glance or a kind word. He stood close to the steps of the Pullman car that she was about to enter, and as she passed him he held out his hand, saying "Good-bye." But he held his hand to no purpose. She was much occupied in taking her valise from the conductor who had hoisted her up, and who was now shouting in stentorian tones "All aboard," though there was not a soul with the slightest intention of boarding the train but herself.

She leaned forward to wave good-bye to Hosmer, and Fanny, and Thérèse, who were on the platform; then she was gone.

Grégoire stood looking stupidly at the vanishing train.

"Are you going back with us?" Hosmer asked him. Fanny and Thérèse had walked ahead.

"No," he replied, looking at Hosmer with ashen face, "I got to go fine my hoss."

VIII

WITH LOOSE REIN

"De Lord be praised fu' de blessin's dat he showers down 'pon us," was Uncle Hiram's graceful conclusion of his supper, after which he pushed his empty plate aside regretfully, and addressed Aunt Belindy. "'Pears to me, Belindy, as you reached a pint wid dem bacon an' greens to-night, dat you never tetched befo'. De pint o' de flavorin' is w'at I alludes to."

"All de same, dat ain't gwine to fetch no mo'," was the rather uncivil reply to this neat compliment to her culinary powers.

"Dah!" cried the youthful Betsy, who formed one of the trio gathered together in the kitchen at Place-du-Bois. "Jis listen (to) Unc' Hiurm! Aunt B'lindy neva tetched a han' to dem bacon an' greens. She tole me out o' her own mouf to put'em on de fiar; she warn't gwine pesta wid 'em."

"Warn't gwine pesta wid 'em?" administering a cuff on the ear of the too communicative Betsy, that sent her sprawling across the table. "T'inks I'se gwine pesta wid you—does you? Messin' roun' heah in de kitchin' an' ain't tu'ned down a bed or drawed a bah, or done a lick o' yo' night wurk yit."

"I is done my night wurk, too," returned Betsy whimpering but defiantly, as she retreated beyond reach of further blows from Aunt Belindy's powerful right hand.

"Dat harshness o' yourn, Belindy, is wat's a sourin' yo' tempa, an' a turnin' of it intur gall an' wormwood. Does you know wat de Scripture tells us of de wrathful woman?"

"Whar I got time to go a foolin' wid Scripture? W'at I wants to know; whar dat Pierson boy, he don't come. He ben gone time 'nough to walk to Natch'toches an' back."

"Ain't dat him I years yonda tu de crib?" suggestod Betsy, coming to join Aunt Belindy in the open doorway.

"You heahs mos' too much fu' yo' own good, you does, gal."

But Betsy was right. For soon a tall, slim negro, young and coal black, mounted the stairs and came into the kitchen, where he deposited a meal bag filled with various necessities that he had brought from Centerville. He was one of the dancers who had displayed their skill before Melicent and Grégoire. Uncle Hiram at once accosted him.

"Well, Pierson, we jest a ben a wonderin' consarnin' you. W'at was de 'casion o' dat long delay?"

"De 'casion? W'y man alive, I couldn't git a dog gone soul in de town to wait on me."

"Dat boy kin lie, yas," said Aunt Belindy, "God A'mighty knows ever time I ben to Centaville dem sto' keepas ain't done a blessed t'ing but settin' down."

"Settin' down—Lord! dey warn't settin' down to-day; you heah me."

"W'at dey doin' ef dey ain't settin' down, Unc' Pierson?" asked Betsy with amiable curiosity.

"You jis drap dat 'uncle,' you," turning wrathfully upon the girl, "sence w'en you start dat new trick?"

"Lef de chile 'lone, Pierson, lef 'er alone. Come heah, Betsy, an' set by yo' Uncle Hiurm."

From the encouraging nearness of Uncle Hiram, she ventured to ask "w'at you 'low dey doin' ef dey ain't settin' down?" this time without adding the offensive title.

"Dey flyin' 'roun', Lord! dey hidin' dey sef! dey gittin' out o' de way, I tell you. Grégor jis ben a raisin' ole Cain in Centaville."

"I know'd it; could a' tole you dat mese'f. My Lan'! but dats a piece, dat Grégor," Aunt Belindy enunciated between paroxysms of laughter, seating herself with her fat arms resting on her knees, and her whole bearing announcing pleased anticipation.

"Dat boy neva did have no car' fur de salvation o' his soul," groaned Uncle Hiram.

"W'at he ben a doin' yonda?" demanded Aunt Belindy impatiently.

"Well," said Pierson, assuming a declamatory air and position in the middle of the large kitchen, "he lef' heah—w'at time he lef heah, Aunt B'lindy?"

"He done lef' fo' dinna, 'caze I seed 'im a lopin' to'ads de riva, time I flung dat Sampson boy out o' de doo', bringin' dem greens in heah 'dout washin' of 'em."

"Dat's so; it war good dinna time w'en he come a lopin' in town. Dat hoss look like he ben swimmin' in Cane Riva, he done ride him so hard. He fling he se'f down front o' Grammont's sto' an' he come a stompin' in, look like gwine hu't somebody. Ole Grammont tell him, 'How you come on, Grégor? Come ova tu de house an' eat dinna wid us: de ladies be pleas tu see you.'"

"Humph," muttered Aunt Belindy, "dem Grammont gals be glad to see any t'ing dat got breeches on; lef 'lone good lookin' piece like dat Grégor."

"Grégor, he neva sey, 'Tank you dog,' jis' fling he big dolla down on de counta an' 'low 'don't want no dinna: gimme some w'iskey.'"

"Yas, yas, Lord," from Aunt Belindy.

"Ole Grammont, he push de bottle to'ads 'im, an' I 'clar to Goodness ef he didn' mos fill dat tumbla to de brim, an' drink it down, neva blink a eye. Den he tu'n an treat ev'y las' w'ite man stan'in' roun'; dat ole kiarpenta man; de blacksmif; Marse Verdon. He keep on a treatin'; Grammont, he keep a handin' out de w'iskey; Grégor he keep on a drinkin' an a treatin'—Grammont, he keep a handin' out; don't make no odds tu him s'long uz dat bring de money in de draw. I ben a stan'in' out on de gallery, me, a peekin' in. An' Grégor, he cuss and swar an' he kiarry on, an 'low he want play game poka. Den dey all goes a trompin' in de back room an' sets down roun' de table, an' I comes a creepin' in, me, whar I kin look frough de doo', an dar dey sets an' plays an Grégor, he drinks w'iskey an' he wins de money. An' arta w'ile Marse Verdon, he little eyes blinkin', he 'low, 'y' all had a shootin' down tu Place-du-Bois, *hein* Grégor?' Grégor, he neva say nuttin': he jis' draw he pistol slow out o' he pocket an' lay it down on de table; an' he look squar in Marse Verdon eyes. Man! ef you eva seed some pussun tu'n' w'ite!"

"Reckon dat heifa 'Milky' look black side li'le Verdon dat time," chuckled Aunt Belindy.

"Jis' uz w'ite uz Unc' Hiurm's shurt an' a trimblin', an' neva say no mo' 'bout shootin'. Den ole Grammont, he kine o' hang back an' say, 'You git de jestice de peace, 'hine you, kiarrin' conceal' weepons dat a-way, Grégor.'"

"Dat ole Grammont, he got to git he gab in ef he gwine die fu' it," interrupted Aunt Belindy.

"Grégor say—'I don't 'lows to kiarr no conceal' weepons,' an he draw nudda pistol slow out o' he udda pocket an' lay et on de table. By dat time he gittin' all de money, he crammin' de money in he pocket; an' dem fellas dey gits up one arta d'udda kine o' shy-like, an' sneaks out. Den Grégor, he git up an come out o' de room, he coat 'crost he arm, an' de pistols a stickin' out an him lookin' sassy tell ev'y body make way, same ef he ben Jay Goul'. Ef he look one o' 'em in de eye dey outs wid, 'Howdy, Grégor—how you come on, Grégor?' jis' uz pelite uz a peacock, an' him neva take no trouble to yansa 'em. He jis' holla out fu' somebody bring dat hoss tu de steps, an' him stan'in' 's big uz life, waitin'. I gits tu de hoss fus', me, an' leads 'im up, an' he gits top dat hoss stidy like he ain't tetch a drap, an' he fling me big dolla."

"Whar de dolla, Mista Pierson?" enquired Betsy.

"De dolla in my pocket, an' et gwine stay dah. Didn' ax you fu' no 'Mista Pierson.' Whar yu' all tink he went on dat hoss?"

"How you reckon we knows whar he wint; we wasn't dah," replied Aunt Belindy.

"He jis' went a lopin' twenty yards down to Chartrand's sto'. I goes on 'hine 'im see w'at he gwine do. Dah he git down f'um de hoss an' go a stompin' in de sto'—eve'ybody stan'in' back jis' same like fu' Jay Goul', an' he fling bill down on de counta an' 'low, 'Fill me up a bottle, Chartrand, I'se gwine travelin'.' Den he 'lows, 'You treats eve'y las' man roun' heah at my 'spence, black an' w'ite—nuttin' fu' me,' an' he fole he arms an' lean back on de counta, jis' so. Chartrand, he look skeerd, he say 'François gwine wait on you.' But Grégor, he 'low he don't wants no rusty skileton a waitin' on him w'en he treat, 'Wait on de gemmen yo'se'f—step up gemmen.' Chartrand 'low, 'Damn ef nigga gwine drink wid w'ite man in dat sto',' all same he kine git 'hine box tu say dat."

"Lord, Lord, de ways o' de transgressor!" groaned Uncle Hiram.

"You want to see dem niggas sneaking 'way," resumed Pierson, "dey knows Grégor gwine fo'ce 'em drink; dey knows Chartrand gwine make it hot fu' 'em art'ards ef dey does. Grégor he spie me jis' I'se tryin' glide frough de doo' an he call out, 'Yonda a gemmen f'um Place-du-Bois; Pierson, come heah; you'se good 'nough tu drink wid any w'ite man, 'cept me; you come heah, take drink wid Mr. Louis Chartrand.'

"I 'lows don't wants no drink, much 'bleege, Marse Grégor'. 'Yis, you wants drink,' an' 'id dat he draws he pistol. 'Mista Chartrand want drink, too. I done owe Mista Chartrand somethin' dis long time; I'se gwine pay 'im wid a treat,' he say. Chartrand look like he on fiar, he so red, he so mad, he swell up same like ole bull frog."

"Dat make no odd," chuckled Aunt Belindy, "he gwine drink wid nigga ef Grégor say so."

"Yes, he drink, Lord, only he cuss me slow, an' 'low he gwine break my skull."

"Lordy! I knows you was jis' a trimblin', Mista Pierson."

"Warn't trimblin' no mo' 'en I'se trimblin' dis minute, an' you drap dat 'Mista.' Den w'at you reckon? Yonda come Père Antoine; he come an' stan' in de doo' an' he hole up he han'; look like he ain't 'feard no body an' he 'low: 'Grégor Sanchun, how is you dar' come in dis heah peaceful town frowin' of it into disorda an' confusion? Ef you isn't 'feard o' man; hasn't you got no fear o' God A'mighty wat punishes?'"

"Grégor, he look at 'im an' he say cool like, 'Howdy, Père Antoine; how you come on?' He got he pistol w'at he draw fu' make Chartrand drink wid dis heah nigga,—he foolin' wid it an' a rubbin' it up and down he pants, an' he 'low 'Dis a gemmen w'at fit to drink wid a Sanchun— w'at'll you have?' But Père Antoine, he go on makin' a su'mon same like he make in chu'ch, an' Grégor, he lean he two arm back on de counta— kine o' smilin' like, an' he say, 'Chartrand, whar dat bottle I orda you put up?' Chartrand bring de bottle; Grégor, he put de bottle in he coat pocket wat hang on he arm—car'ful.

"Père Antoine, he go on preachin', he say, 'I tell you dis young man, you 'se on de big road w'at leads tu hell.'

"Den Grégor straight he se'f up an' walk close to Père Antoine an' he say, 'Hell an' damnation dar ain't no sich a place. I reckon she know; w'at you know side o' her. She say dar ain't no hell, an' ef you an' de Archbishop an' de Angel Gabriel come along an' 'low dey a hell, you all liars,' an' he say, 'Make way dah, I'se a gittin' out o' heah; dis ain't no town fittin' to hol' a Sanchun. Make way ef you don' wants to go to Kingdom come fo' yo' time.'

"Well, I 'lows dey did make way. Only Père Antoine, he look mighty sorry an' down cas'.

"Grégor go out dat sto' taking plenty room, an' walkin' car'ful like, an' he swing he se'f on de hoss; den he lean down mos' flat an' stick he spurs in dat hoss an' he go tar'in' like de win' down street, out o' de town, a firin' he pistol up in de a'r."

Uncle Hiram had listened to the foregoing recital with troubled countenance, and with many a protesting groan. He now shook his old white head, and heaved a deep sigh. "All dat gwine come hard an' heavy on de madam. She don't desarve it—God knows, she don't desarve it."

"How you, ole like you is, kin look fu' somethin' diffunt, Unc' Hiurm?" observed Aunt Belindy philosophically. "Don't you know Grégor gwine be Grégor tell he die? Dat's all dar is 'bout it."

Betsy arose with the sudden recollection that she had let the time pass for bringing in Miss Thérèse's hot water, and Pierson went to the stove to see what Aunt Belindy had reserved for him in the shape of supper.

IX

The Reason Why

S ampson, the young colored boy who had lighted Fanny's fire on the first day of her arrival at Place-du-Bois, and who had made such insinuating advances of friendliness towards her, had continued to attract her notice and good will. He it was who lighted her fires on such mornings as they were needed. For there had been no winter. In mid-January, the grass was fresh and green; trees and plants were putting forth tender shoots, as if in welcome to spring; roses were blossoming, and it was a veritable atmosphere of Havana rather than of central Louisiana that the dwellers at Place-du-Bois were enjoying. But finally winter made tardy assertion of its rights. One morning broke raw and black with an icy rain falling, and young Sampson arriving in the early bleakness to attend to his duties at the cottage, presented a picture of human distress to move the most hardened to pity. Though dressed comfortably in the clothing with which Fanny had apparelled him— he was ashen. Save for the chattering of his teeth, his body seemed possessed of a paralytic inability to move. He knelt before the empty fire-place as he had done on that first day, and with deep sighs and groans went about his work. Then he remained long before the warmth that he had kindled; even lying full length upon the soft rug, to bask in the generous heat that permeated and seemed to thaw his stiffened limbs.

Next, he went quietly into the bedroom to attend to the fire there. Hosmer and Fanny were still sleeping. He approached a decorated basket that hung against the wall; a receptacle for old newspapers and odds and ends. He drew something from his rather capacious coat pocket, and, satisfying himself that Hosmer slept, thrust it in the bottom of the basket, well covered by the nondescript accumulation that was there.

The house was very warm and cheerful when they arose, and after breakfasting Hosmer felt unusually reluctant to quit his fire-side and face the inclement day; for an unaccustomed fatigue hung upon his limbs and his body was sore, as from the effect of bruises. But he went, nevertheless, well encased in protective rubber; and as he turned away from the house, Fanny hastened to the hanging basket, and fumbling nervously in its depths, found what the complaisant Sampson had left for her.

The cold rain had gradually changed into a fine mist, that in descending, spread an icy coat upon every object that it touched. When Hosmer returned at noon, he did not leave the house again.

During the afternoon Thérèse knocked at Fanny's door. She was enveloped in a long hooded cloak, her face glowing from contact with the sharp moist air, and myriad crystal drops clinging to her fluffy blonde hair that looked very golden under the dark hood that covered it. She wanted to learn how Fanny accepted this unpleasant change of atmospheric conditions, intending to bear her company for the remainder of the day if she found her depressed, as was often the case.

"Why, I didn't know you were home," she said, a little startled, to Hosmer who opened the door to her. "I came over to show Mrs. Hosmer something pretty that I don't suppose she ever saw before." It was a branch from a rose-tree, bearing two open blossoms and a multitude of buds, creamy pink, all encased in an icy transparency that gleamed like diamonds. "Isn't it exquisite?" she said, holding the spray up for Fanny's admiration. But she saw at a glance that the spirit of Disorder had descended and settled upon the Hosmer household.

The usually neat room was in a sad state of confusion. Some of the pictures had been taken from the walls, and were leaning here and there against chairs and tables. The mantel ornaments had been removed and deposited at random and in groups about the room. On the hearth was a pail of water in which swam a huge sponge; and Fanny sat beside the center-table that was piled with her husband's wearing apparel, holding in her lap a coat which she had evidently been passing under inspection. Her hair had escaped from its fastenings; her collar was hooked awry; her face was flushed and her whole bearing indicated her condition.

Hosmer took the frozen spray from Thérèse's hand, and spoke a little about the beauty of the trees, especially the young cedars that he had passed out in the hills on his way home.

"It's all well and good to talk about flowers and things, Mrs. Laferm— sit down please—but when a person's got the job that I've got on my hands, she's something else to think about. And David here smoking one cigar after another. He knows all I've got to do, and goes and sends those darkies home right after dinner."

Thérèse was so shocked that for a while she could say nothing; till for Hosmer's sake she made a quick effort to appear at ease.

"What have you to do, Mrs. Hosmer? Let me help you, I can give you the whole afternoon," she said with an appearance of being ready for any thing that was at hand to be done.

Fanny turned the coat over in her lap, and looked down helplessly at a stain on the collar, that she had been endeavoring to remove; at the same time pushing aside with patient repetition the wisp of hair that kept falling over her cheek.

"Belle Worthington'll be here before we know it; her and her husband and that Lucilla of hers. David knows how Belle Worthington is, just as well as I do; there's no use saying he don't. If she was to see a speck of dirt in this house or on David's clothes, or anything, why we'd never hear the last of it. I got a letter from her," she continued, letting the coat fall to the floor, whilst she endeavored to find her pocket.

"Is she coming to visit you?" asked Thérèse who had taken up a feather brush, and was dusting and replacing the various ornaments that were scattered through the room.

"She's going down to Muddy Graw (Mardi-Gras) her and her husband and Lucilla and she's going to stop here a while. I had that letter—I guess I must of left it in the other room."

"Never mind," Thérèse hastened to say, seeing that her whole energies were centered on finding the letter.

"Let me look," said Hosmer, making a movement towards the bedroom door, but Fanny had arisen and holding out a hand to detain him she went into the room herself, saying she knew where she'd left it.

"Is this the reason you've kept yourself shut up here in the house so often?" Thérèse asked of Hosmer, drawing near him. "Never telling me a word of it," she went on, "it wasn't right; it wasn't kind."

"Why should I have put any extra burden on you?" he answered, looking down at her, and feeling a joy in her presence there, that seemed like a guilty indulgence in face of his domestic shame.

"Don't stay," Thérèse said. "Leave me here. Go to your office or over to the house—leave me alone with her."

Fanny returned, having found the letter, and spoke with increased vehemence of the necessity of having the house in perfect trim against the arrival of Belle Worthington, from whom they would never hear the last, and so forth.

"Well, your husband is going out, and that will give us a chance to get things righted," said Thérèse encouragingly. "You know men are always in the way at such times."

"It's what he ought to done before; and left Suze and Minervy here," she replied with grudging acquiescence.

After repeated visits to the bedroom, under various pretexts, Fanny grew utterly incapable to do more than sit and gaze stupidly at Thérèse, who busied herself in bringing the confusion of the sitting-room into some order.

She continued to talk disjointedly of Belle Worthington and her well known tyrannical characteristics in regard to cleanliness; finishing by weeping mildly at the prospect of her own inability to ever reach the high standard required by her exacting friend.

It was far in the afternoon—verging upon night, when Thérèse succeeded in persuading her that she was ill and should go to bed. She gladly seized upon the suggestion of illness; assuring Thérèse that she alone had guessed her affliction: that whatever was thought singular in her behavior must be explained by that sickness which was past being guessed at—then she went to bed.

It was late when Hosmer left his office; a rough temporary shanty, put together near the ruined mill.

He started out slowly on his long cold ride. His physical malaise of the morning had augmented as the day went on, and he was beginning to admit to himself that he was "in for it."

But the cheerless ride was lightened by a picture that had been with him through the afternoon, and that moved him in his whole being, as the moment approached when it might be changed to reality. He knew Fanny's habits; knew that she would be sleeping now. Thérèse would not leave her there alone in the house—of that he was sure. And he pictured Thérèse at this moment seated at his fire-side. He would find her there when he entered. His heart beat tumultuously at the thought. It was a very weak moment with him, possibly, one in which his unnerved condition stood for some account. But he felt that when he saw her there, waiting for him, he would cast himself at her feet and kiss them. He would crush her white hands against his bosom. He would bury his face in her silken hair. She should know how strong his love was, and he would hold her in his arms till she yield back tenderness to his own. But—Thérèse met him on the steps. As he was mounting them, she was descending; wrapped in her long cloak, her pretty head covered by the dark hood.

"Oh, are you going?" he asked.

She heard the note of entreaty in his voice.

"Yes," she answered, "I shouldn't have left her before you came; but I knew you were here; I heard your horse's tread a moment ago. She's asleep. Good night. Take courage and have a brave heart," she said, pressing his hand a moment in both hers, and was gone.

The room was as he had pictured it; order restored and the fire blazing brightly. On the table was a pot of hot tea and a tempting little supper laid. But he pushed it all aside and buried his face down upon the table into his folded arms, groaning aloud. Physical suffering; thwarted love, and at the same time a feeling of self-condemnation, made him wish that life were ended for him.

Fanny awoke close upon morning, not knowing what had aroused her. She was for a little while all bewildered and unable to collect herself. She soon learned the cause of her disturbance. Hosmer was tossing about and his outstretched arm lay across her face, where it had evidently been flung with some violence. She took his hand to move it away, and it burned her like a coal of fire. As she touched him he started and began to talk incoherently. He evidently fancied himself dictating a letter to some insurance company, in no pleased terms—of which Fanny caught but snatches. Then:

"That's too much, Mrs. Lafirme; too much—too much—Don't let Grégoire burn—take him from the fire, some one. Thirty day's credit—shipment made on tenth," he rambled on at intervals in his troubled sleep.

Fanny trembled with apprehension as she heard him. Surely he has brain fever she thought, and she laid her hand gently on his burning forehead. He covered it with his own, muttering "Thérèse, Thérèse—so good—let me love you."

X

Perplexing Things

"Lucilla!"

The pale, drooping girl started guiltily at her mother's sharp exclamation, and made an effort to throw back her shoulders. Then she bit her nails nervously, but soon desisted, remembering that that also, as well as yielding to a relaxed tendency of the spinal column, was a forbidden indulgence.

"Put on your hat and go on out and get a breath of fresh air; you're as white as milk-man's cream."

Lucilla rose and obeyed her mother's order with the precision of a soldier, following the directions of his commander.

"How submissive and gentle your daughter is," remarked Thérèse.

"Well, she's got to be, and she knows it. Why, I haven't got to do more than look at that girl most times for her to understand what I want. You didn't notice, did you, how she straightened up when I called 'Lucilla' to her? She knows by the tone of my voice what she's got to do."

"Most mothers can't boast of having such power over their daughters."

"Well, I'm not the woman to stand any shenanigans from a child of mine. I could name you dead loads of women that are just completely walked over by their children. It's a blessing that boy of Fanny's died, between you and I; its what I've always said. Why, Mrs. Laferm, she couldn't any more look after a youngster than she could after a baby elephant. By the by, what do you guess is the matter with her, any way?"

"How, the matter?" Thérèse asked; the too ready blood flushing her face and neck as she laid down her work and looked up at Mrs. Worthington.

"Why, she's acting mighty queer, that's all I can say for her."

"I haven't been able to see her for some time," Thérèse returned, going back to her sewing, "but I suppose she got a little upset and nervous over her husband; he had a few days of very serious illness before you came."

"Oh, I've seen her in all sorts of states and conditions, and I've never seen her like that before. Why, she does nothing in the God's world but whine and sniffle, and wish she was dead; it's enough to give a person the horrors. She can't make out she's sick; I never saw her look better in my life. She must of gained ten pounds since she come down here."

"Yes," said Thérèse, "she was looking so well, and—and I thought everything was going well with her too, but—" and she hesitated to go on.

"Oh, I know what you want to say. You can't help that. No use bothering your brains about that—now you just take my advice," exclaimed Mrs. Worthington brusquely.

Then she laughed so loud and suddenly that Thérèse, being already nervous, pricked her finger with her needle till the blood came; a mishap which decided her to lay aside her work.

"If you never saw a fish out of water, Mrs. Laferm, do take a peep at Mr. Worthington astride that horse; it's enough to make a cat expire!"

Mrs. Worthington was on the whole rather inclined to take her husband seriously. As often as he might excite her disapproval, it was seldom that he aroused her mirth. So it may be gathered that his appearance in this unfamiliar rôle of horseman was of the most mirth-provoking.

He and Hosmer were dismounting at the cottage, which decided Mrs. Worthington to go and look after them; Fanny for the time being—in her opinion—not having "the gumption to look after a sick kitten."

"This is what I call solid comfort," she said looking around the well appointed sitting-room, before quitting it.

"You ought to be a mighty happy woman, Mrs. Laferm; only I'd think you'd die of lonesomeness, sometimes."

Thérèse laughed, and told her not to forget that she expected them all over in the evening.

"You can depend on me; and I'll do my best to drag Fanny over; so-long."

When left alone, Thérèse at once relapsed into the gloomy train of reflections that had occupied her since the day she had seen with her bodily eyes something of the wretched life that she had brought upon the man she loved. And yet that wretchedness in its refinement of cruelty and immorality she could not guess and was never to know. Still, she had seen enough to cause her to ask herself with a shudder "was I right—was I right?"

She had always thought this lesson of right and wrong a very plain one. So easy of interpretation that the simplest minded might solve it if they would. And here had come for the first time in her life a staggering doubt as to its nature. She did not suspect that she was submitting one of those knotty problems to her unpracticed judgment that philosophers and theologians delight in disagreeing upon, and her inability to unravel it staggered her. She tried to convince herself that a very insistent sting of remorse which she felt, came from selfishness—from the pain that her own heart suffered in the knowledge of Hosmer's unhappiness. She was not callous enough to quiet her soul with the balm of having intended the best. She continued to ask herself only "was I right?" and it was by the answer to that question that she would abide, whether in the stony content of accomplished righteousness, or in an enduring remorse that pointed to a goal in whose labyrinthine possibilities her soul lost itself and fainted away.

Lucilla went out to get a breath of fresh air as her mother had commanded, but she did not go far to seek it. Not further than the end of the back veranda, where she stood for some time motionless, before beginning to occupy herself in a way which Aunt Belindy, who was watching her from the kitchen window, considered highly problematical. The negress was wiping a dish and giving it a fine polish in her absence of mind. When her curiosity could no longer contain itself she called out:

"W'ats dat you'se doin' dah, you li'le gal? Come heah an' le' me see." Lucilla turned with the startled look which seemed to be usual with her when addressed.

"Le' me see," repeated Aunt Belindy pleasantly.

Lucilla approached the window and handed the woman a small square of stiff writing paper which was stuck with myriad tiny pin-holes; some of which she had been making when interrupted by Aunt Belindy.

"W'at in God A'Mighty's name you call dat 'ar?" the darkey asked examining the paper critically, as though expecting the riddle would solve itself before her eyes.

"Those are my acts I've been counting," the girl replied a little gingerly.

"Yo' ax? I don' see nuttin' 'cep' a piece o' papah plum fill up wid holes. W'at you call ax?"

"Acts—acts. Don't you know what acts are?"

"How you want me know? I neva ben to no school whar you larn all dat."

"Why, an act is something you do that you don't want to do—or something you don't want to do, that you do—I mean that you don't do. Or if you want to eat something and don't. Or an aspiration; that's an act, too."

"Go long! W'ats dat—aspiration?"

"Why, to say any kind of little prayer; or if you invoke our Lord, or our Blessed Lady, or one of the saints, that's an aspiration. You can make them just as quick as you can think—you can make hundreds and hundreds in a day."

"My Lan'! Dat's w'at you'se studyin' 'bout w'en you'se steppin' 'roun' heah like a droopy pullet? An' I t'ought you was studyin' 'bout dat beau you lef' yonda to Sent Lous."

"You mustn't say such things to me; I'm going to be a religious."

"How dat gwine henda you have a beau ef you'se religious?"

"The religious never get married," turning very red, "and don't live in the world like others."

"Look heah, chile, you t'inks I'se fool? Religion—no religion, whar you gwine live ef you don' live in de word? Gwine live up in de moon?"

"You're a very ignorant person," replied Lucilla, highly offended. "A religious devotes her life to God, and lives in the convent."

"Den w'y you neva said 'convent'? I knows all 'bout convent. W'at you gwine do wid dem ax w'en de papah done all fill up?" handing the singular tablet back to her.

"Oh," replied Lucilla, "when I have thousands and thousands I gain twenty-five years' indulgence."

"Is dat so?"

"Yes," said the girl; and divining that Aunt Belindy had not understood, "twenty-five years that I don't have to go to purgatory. You see most people have to spend years and years in purgatory, before they can get to Heaven."

"How you know dat?"

If Aunt Belindy had asked Lucilla how she knew that the sun shone, she could not have answered with more assurance "because I know" as she turned and walked rather scornfully away.

"W'at dat kine o' fool talk dey larns gals up yonda tu Sent Lous? An' huh ma a putty woman; yas, bless me; all dress up fittin' to kill. Don' 'pear like she studyin' 'bout ax."

XI

A Social Evening

M r. and Mrs. Joseph Duplan with their little daughter Ninette, who had been invited to Place-du-Bois for supper, as well as for the evening, were seated with Thérèse in the parlor, awaiting the arrival of the cottage guests. They had left their rather distant plantation, Les Chênières, early in the afternoon, wishing as usual to make the most of these visits, which, though infrequent, were always so much enjoyed.

The room was somewhat altered since that summer day when Thérèse had sat in its cool shadows, hearing the story of David Hosmer's life. Only with such difference, however, as the change of season called for; imparting to it a rich warmth that invited to sociability and friendly confidences. In the depths of the great chimney glowed with a steady and dignified heat, the huge back-log, whose disposal Uncle Hiram had superintended in person; and the leaping flames from the dry hickories that surrounded it, lent a very genial light to the grim-visaged Lafirmes who looked down from their elevation on the interesting group gathered about the hearth.

Conversation had never once flagged with these good friends; for, aside from much neighborhood gossip to be told and listened to, there was the always fertile topic of "crops" to be discussed in all its bearings, that touched, in its local and restricted sense, the labor question, cultivation, freight rates, and the city merchant.

With Mrs. Duplan there was a good deal to be said about the unusual mortality among "Plymouth-Rocks" owing to an alarming prevalence of "pip," which malady, however, that lady found to be gradually yielding to a heroic treatment introduced into her *basse-cour* by one Coulon, a piney wood sage of some repute as a mystic healer.

This was a delicate refined little woman, somewhat old-fashioned and stranded in her incapability to keep pace with the modern conduct of life; but giving her views with a pretty self-confidence, that showed her a ruler in her peculiar realm.

The young Ninette had extended herself in an easy chair, in an attitude of graceful abandonment, the earnest brown eyes looking eagerly out from under a tangle of auburn hair, and resting with absorbed admiration upon her father, whose words and movements she followed with unflagging attentiveness. The fastidious little miss was clad in a dainty gown that reached scarcely below the knees; revealing the shapely limbs that were crossed and extended to let the well shod feet rest upon the polished brass fender.

Thérèse had given what information lay within her range, concerning the company which was expected. But her confidences had plainly been insufficient to prepare Mrs. Duplan for the startling effect produced by Mrs. Worthington on that little woman in her black silk of a by-gone fashion; so splendid was Mrs. Worthington's erect and imposing figure, so blonde her blonde hair, so bright her striking color and so comprehensive the sweep of her blue and scintillating gown. Yet was Mrs. Worthington not at ease, as might be noticed in the unnatural quaver of her high-pitched voice and the restless motion of her hands, as she seated herself with an arm studiedly resting upon the table near by.

Hosmer had met the Duplans before; on the occasion of a former visit to Place-du-Bois and again at Les Chênières when he had gone to see the planter on business connected with the lumber trade.

Fanny was a stranger to them and promised to remain such; for she acknowledged her presentation with a silent bow and retreated as far from the group as a decent concession to sociability would permit.

Thérèse with her pretty Creole tact was not long in bringing these seemingly incongruent elements into some degree of harmony. Mr. Duplan in his courteous and rather lordly way was presently imparting to Mrs. Worthington certain reminiscences of a visit to St. Louis twenty-five years before, when he and Mrs. Duplan had rather hastily traversed that interesting town during their wedding journey. Mr. Duplan's manner had a singular effect upon Mrs. Worthington, who became dignified, subdued, and altogether unnatural in her endeavor to adjust herself to it.

Mr. Worthington seated himself beside Mrs. Duplan and was soon trying to glean information, in his eager short-sighted way, of psychological interest concerning the negro race; such effort rather bewildering that good lady, who could not bring herself to view the negro as an interesting or suitable theme to be introduced into polite conversation.

Hosmer sat and talked good-naturedly to the little girls, endeavoring to dispel the shyness with which they seemed inclined to view each other—and Thérèse crossed the room to join Fanny.

"I hope you're feeling better," she ventured, "you should have let me help you while Mr. Hosmer was ill."

Fanny looked away, biting her lip, the sudden tears coming to her eyes. She answered with unsteady voice, "Oh, I was able to look after my husband myself, Mrs. Laferm."

Thérèse reddened at finding herself so misunderstood. "I meant in your housekeeping, Mrs. Hosmer; I could have relieved you of some of that worry, whilst you were occupied with your husband."

Fanny continued to look unhappy; her features taking on that peculiar downward droop which Thérèse had come to know and mistrust.

"Are you going to New Orleans with Mrs. Worthington?" she asked, "she told me she meant to try and persuade you."

"No; I'm not going. Why?" looking suspiciously in Thérèse's face.

"Well," laughed Thérèse, "only for the sake of asking, I suppose. I thought you'd enjoy Mardi-Gras, never having seen it."

"I'm not going anywheres unless David goes along," she said, with an impertinent ring in her voice, and with a conviction that she was administering a stab and a rebuke. She had come prepared to watch her husband and Mrs. Lafirme, her heart swelling with jealous suspicion as she looked constantly from one to the other, endeavoring to detect signs of an understanding between them. Failing to discover such, and loth to be robbed of her morbid feast of misery, she set her failure down to their pre-determined subtlety. Thérèse was conscious of a change in Fanny's attitude, and felt herself unable to account for it otherwise than by whim, which she knew played a not unimportant rôle in directing the manner of a large majority of women. Moreover, it was not a moment to lose herself in speculation concerning this woman's capricious behavior. Her guests held the first claim upon her attentions. Indeed, here was Mrs. Worthington even now loudly demanding a pack of cards. "Here's a gentleman never heard of six-handed euchre. If you've got a pack of cards, Mrs. Laferm, I guess I can show him quick enough that it can be done."

"Oh, I don't doubt Mrs. Worthington's ability to make any startling and pleasing revelations," rejoined the planter good humoredly, and gallantly following Mrs. Worthington who had risen with the view of putting into immediate effect her scheme of initiating these slow people into the unsuspected possibilities of euchre; a game which, however adaptable in other ways, could certainly not be indulged in by seven persons. After each one proffering, as is usual on such occasions, his readiness to assume the character of on-looker, Mr. Worthington's claim to entire indifference, if not inability—confirmed by his wife—was accepted as the most sincere, and that gentleman was excluded and excused.

He watched them as they seated themselves at table, even lending assistance, in his own awkward way, to range the chairs in place. Then he followed the game for a while, standing behind Fanny to note the outcome of her reckless offer of "five on hearts," with only three trumps in hand, and every indication of little assistance from her partners, Mr. Duplan and Belle Worthington.

At one end of the room was a long, low, well-filled book-case. Here had been the direction of Mr. Worthington's secret and stolen glances the entire evening. And now towards this point he finally transported himself by gradual movements which he believed appeared unstudied and indifferent. He was confronted by a good deal of French—to him an unfamiliar language. Here a long row of Balzac; then, the Waverley Novels in faded red cloth of very old date. Racine, Moliere, Bulwer following in more modern garb; Shakespeare in a compass that promised very small type. His quick trained glance sweeping along the shelves, contracted into a little frown of resentment while he sent his hand impetuously through his scant locks, standing them quite on end.

On the very lowest shelf were five imposing volumes in dignified black and gold, bearing the simple inscription "Lives of the Saints—Rev. A. Butler." Upon one of them, Mr. Worthington seized, opening it at hazard. He had fallen upon the history of St. Monica, mother of the great St. Austin—a woman whose habits it appears had been so closely guarded in her childhood by a pious nurse, that even the quenching of her natural thirst was permitted only within certain well defined bounds. This mentor used to say "you are now for drinking water, but when you come to be mistress of the cellar, water will be despised, but the habit of drinking will stick by you." Highly interesting, Mr. Worthington thought, as he brushed his hair all down again the right way and seated himself the better to learn the fortunes of the good St. Monica who, curiously enough, notwithstanding those early incentives to temperance, "insensibly contracted an inclination to wine," drinking "whole cups of it with pleasure as it came in her way." A "dangerous intemperance" which it finally pleased Heaven to cure through the instrumentality of a maid servant taunting her mistress with being a "wine bibber."

Mr. Worthington did not stop with the story of Saint Monica. He lost himself in those details of asceticism, martyrdom, superhuman possibilities which man is capable of attaining under peculiar conditions of life—something he had not yet "gone into."

The voices at the card table would certainly have disturbed a man with less power of mind concentration. For Mrs. Worthington in this familiar employment was herself again—*con fuoco*. Here was Mr. Duplan in high spirits; his wife putting forth little gushes of bird-like exaltation as the fascinations of the game revealed themselves to her. Even Hosmer and Thérèse were drawn for the moment from their usual preoccupation. Fanny alone was the ghost of the feast. Her features never relaxed from their settled gloom. She played at hap-hazard, listlessly throwing down the cards or letting them fall from her hands, vaguely asking what were trumps at inopportune moments; showing that inattentiveness so exasperating to an eager player and which oftener than once drew a sharp rebuke from Belle Worthington.

"Don't you wish we could play," said Ninette to her companion from her comfortable perch beside the fire, and looking longingly towards the card table.

"Oh, no," replied Lucilla briefly, gazing into the fire, with hands folded in her lap. Thin hands, showing up very white against the dull colored "convent uniform" that hung in plain, severe folds about her and reached to her very ankles.

"Oh, don't you? I play often at home when company comes. And I play cribbage and *vingt-et-un* with papa and win lots of money from him."

"That's wrong."

"No, it isn't; papa wouldn't do it if it was wrong," she answered decidedly. "Do you go to the convent?" she asked, looking critically at Lucilla and drawing a little nearer, so as to be confidential. "Tell me about it," she continued, when the other had replied affirmatively. "Is it very dreadful? you know they're going to send me soon."

"Oh, it's the best place in the world," corrected Lucilla as eagerly as she could.

"Well, mamma says she was just as happy as could be there, but you see that's so awfully long ago. It must have changed since then."

"The convent never changes: it's always the same. You first go to chapel to mass early in the morning."

"Ugh!" shuddered Ninette.

"Then you have studies," continued Lucilla. "Then breakfast, then recreation, then classes, and there's meditation."

"Oh, well," interrupted Ninette, "I believe anything most would suit you, and mamma when she was little; but if I don't like it—see here, if I tell you something will you promise never, never, to tell?"

"Is it any thing wrong?"

"Oh, no, not very; it isn't a real mortal sin. Will you promise?"

"Yes," agreed Lucilla; curiosity getting something the better of her pious scruples.

"Cross your heart?"

Lucilla crossed her heart carefully, though a little reluctantly.

"Hope you may die?"

"Oh!" exclaimed the little convent girl aghast.

"Oh, pshaw," laughed Ninette, "never mind. But that's what Polly always says when she wants me to believe her: 'hope I may die, Miss Ninette.' Well, this is it: I've been saving up money for the longest time, oh ever so long. I've got eighteen dollars and sixty cents, and when they send me to the convent, if I don't like it, I'm going to run away." This last and startling revelation was told in a tragic whisper in Lucilla's ear, for Betsy was standing before them with a tray of chocolate and coffee that she was passing around.

"I yeard you," proclaimed Betsy with mischievous inscrutable countenance.

"You didn't," said Ninette defiantly, and taking a cup of coffee.

"Yas, I did, I yeard you," walking away.

"See here, Betsy," cried Ninette recalling the girl, "you're not going to tell, are you?"

"Dun know ef I isn't gwine tell. Dun know ef I isn't gwine tell Miss Duplan dis yere ver' minute."

"Oh Betsy," entreated Ninette, "I'll give you this dress if you don't. I don't want it any more."

Betsy's eyes glowed, but she looked down unconcernedly at the pretty gown.

"Don't spec it fit me. An' you know Miss T'rèse ain't gwine let me go flyin' roun' wid my laigs stickin' out dat away."

"I'll let the ruffle down, Betsy," eagerly proposed Ninette.

"Betsy!" called Thérèse a little impatiently.

"Yas, 'um—I ben waitin' fu' de cups."

Lucilla had made many an aspiration—many an "act" the while. This whole evening of revelry, and now this last act of wicked conspiracy seemed to have tainted her soul with a breath of sin which she would not feel wholly freed from, till she had cleansed her spirit in the waters of absolution.

The party broke up at a late hour, though the Duplans had a long distance to go, and, moreover, had to cross the high and turbid river to reach their carriage which had been left on the opposite bank, owing to the difficulty of the crossing.

Mr. Duplan took occasion of a moment aside to whisper to Hosmer with the air of a connoisseur, "fine woman that Mrs. Worthington of yours."

Hosmer laughed at the jesting implication, whilst disclaiming it, and Fanny looked moodily at them both, jealously wondering at the cause of their good humor.

Mrs. Duplan, under the influence of a charming evening passed in such agreeable and distinguished company, was full of amiable bustle in leaving and had many pleasant parting words to say to each, in her pretty broken English.

"Oh, yes, ma'am," said Mrs. Worthington to that lady, who had taken admiring notice of the beautiful silver "Holy Angels" medal that hung from Lucilla's neck and rested against the dark gown. "Lucilla takes after Mr. Worthington as far as religion goes—kind of different though, for I must say it ain't often he darkens the doors of a church."

Mrs. Worthington always spoke of her husband present as of a husband absent. A peculiarity which he patiently endured, having no talent for repartee, that he had at one time thought of cultivating. But that time was long past.

The Duplans were the first to leave. Then Thérèse stood for a while on the veranda in the chill night air watching the others disappear across the lawn. Mr. and Mrs. Worthington and Lucilla had all shaken hands with her in saying good night. Fanny followed suit limply and grudgingly. Hosmer buttoned his coat impatiently and only lifted his hat to Thérèse as he helped his wife down the stairs.

Poor Fanny! she had already taken exception at that hand pressure which was to come and for which she watched, and now her whole small being was in a jealous turmoil—because there had been none.

XII

Tidings That Sting

Thérèse felt that the room was growing oppressive. She had been sitting all morning alone before the fire, passing in review a great heap of household linen that lay piled beside her on the floor, alternating this occupation with occasional careful and tender offices bestowed upon a wee lamb that had been brought to her some hours before, and that now lay wounded and half lifeless upon a pile of coffee sacks before the blaze.

A fire was hardly needed, except to dispel the dampness that had even made its insistent way indoors, covering walls and furniture with a clammy film. Outside, the moisture was dripping from the glistening magnolia leaves and from the pointed polished leaves of the live-oaks, and the sun that had come out with intense suddenness was drawing it steaming from the shingled roof-tops.

When Thérèse, finally aware of the closeness of the room, opened the door and went out on the veranda, she saw a man, a stranger, riding towards the house and she stood to await his approach. He belonged to what is rather indiscriminately known in that section of the State as the "piney-woods" genus. A rawboned fellow, lank and long of leg; as ungroomed with his scraggy yellow hair and beard as the scrubby little Texas pony which he rode. His big soft felt hat had done unreasonable service as a head-piece; and the "store clothes" that hung upon his lean person could never in their remotest freshness have masqueraded under the character of "all wool." He was in transit, as the bulging saddle-bags that hung across his horse indicated, as well as the rough brown blanket strapped behind him to the animal's back. He rode up close to the rail of the veranda near which Thérèse stood, and nodded to her without offering to raise or touch his hat. She was prepared for the drawl with which he addressed her, and even guessed at what his first words would be.

"You're Mrs. Laferm I 'low?"

Thérèse acknowledged her identity with a bow.

"My name's Jimson; Rufe Jimson," he went on, settling himself on the pony and folding his long knotty hands over the hickory switch that he carried in guise of whip.

"Do you wish to speak to me? won't you dismount?" Thérèse asked.

"I hed my dinner down to the store," he said taking her proposal as an invitation to dine, and turning to expectorate a mouth full of tobacco juice before continuing. "Capital sardines them air," passing his hand over his mouth and beard in unctuous remembrance of the oily dainties.

"I'm just from Cornstalk, Texas, on mu way to Grant. An' them roads as I've traversed isn't what I'd call the best in a fair and square talk."

His manner bore not the slightest mark of deference. He spoke to Thérèse as he might have spoken to one of her black servants, or as he would have addressed a princess of royal blood if fate had ever brought him into such unlikely contact, so clearly was the sense of human equality native to him.

Thérèse knew her animal, and waited patiently for his business to unfold itself.

"I reckon thar hain't no ford hereabouts?" he asked, looking at her with a certain challenge.

"Oh, no; its even difficult crossing in the flat," she answered.

"Wall, I hed calc'lated continooing on this near side. Reckon I could make it?" challenging her again to an answer.

"There's no road on this side," she said, turning away to fasten more securely the escaped branches of a rose-bush that twined about a column near which she stood.

Whether there were a road on this side or on the other side, or no road at all, appeared to be matter of equal indifference to Mr. Jimson, so far as his manner showed. He continued imperturbably "I 'lowed to stop here on a little matter o' business. 'Tis some out o' mu way; more'n I'd calc'lated. You couldn't tell the ixact distance from here to Colfax, could you?"

Thérèse rather impatiently gave him the desired information, and begged that he would disclose his business with her.

"Wall," he said, "onpleasant news 'll keep most times tell you're ready fur it. Thet's my way o' lookin' at it."

"Unpleasant news for me?" she inquired, startled from her indifference and listlessness.

"Rather onpleasant ez I take it. I hain't a makin' no misstatement to persume thet Grégor Sanchun was your nephew?"

"Yes, yes," responded Thérèse, now thoroughly alarmed, and approaching as close to Mr. Rufe Jimson as the dividing rail would permit, "What of him, please?"

He turned again to discharge an accumulation of tobacco juice into a thick border of violets, and resumed.

"You see a hot-blooded young feller, ez wouldn't take no more 'an give no odds, stranger or no stranger in the town, he couldn't ixpect civil treatment; leastways not from Colonel Bill Klayton. Ez I said to Tozier—"

"Please tell me as quickly as possible what has happened," demanded Thérèse with trembling eagerness; steadying herself with both hands on the railing before her.

"You see it all riz out o' a little altercation 'twixt him and Colonel Klayton in the colonel's store. Some says he'd ben drinkin'; others denies it. Howsomever they did hev words risin' out o' the colonel addressing your nephew under the title o' 'Frenchy'; which most takes ez a insufficient cause for rilin'."

"He's dead?" gasped Thérèse, looking at the dispassionate Texan with horrified eyes.

"Wall, yes," an admission which he seemed not yet willing to leave unqualified; for he went on "It don't do to alluz speak out open an' above boards, leastways not thar in Cornstalk. But I'll 'low to you, it's my opinion the colonel acted hasty. It's true 'nough, the young feller hed drawed, but ez I said to Tozier, thet's no reason to persume it was his intention to use his gun."

So Grégoire was dead. She understood it all now. The manner of his death was plain to her as if she had seen it, out there in some disorderly settlement. Killed by the hand of a stranger with whom perhaps the taking of a man's life counted as little as it had once counted with his victim. This flood of sudden and painful intelligence staggered her, and leaning against the column she covered her eyes with both hands, for a while forgetting the presence of the man who had brought the sad tidings.

But he had never ceased his monotonous unwinding. "Thar hain't no manner o' doubt, marm," he was saying, "thet he did hev the sympathy o' the intire community—ez far ez they was free to express it—barrin' a few. Fur he was a likely young chap, that warn't no two opinions o' that. Free with his money—alluz ready to set up fur a friend. Here's a bit o' writin' thet'll larn you more o' the pertic'lars," drawing a letter from his pocket, "writ by the Catholic priest, by name of O'Dowd. He 'lowed you mought want proyer meetin's and sich."

"Masses," corrected Thérèse, holding out her hand for the letter. With the other hand she was wiping away the tears that had gathered thick in her eyes.

"Thar's a couple more little tricks thet he sont," continued Rufe Jimson, apparently dislocating his joints to reach the depths of his trouser pocket, from which he drew a battered pocket book wrapped around with an infinity of string. From the grimy folds of this receptacle he took a small paper parcel which he placed in her hand. It was partly unfastened, and as she opened it fully, the pent-up tears came blindingly—for before her lay a few curling rings of soft brown hair, and a pair of scapulars, one of which was pierced by a tell-tale bullet hole.

"Won't you dismount?" she presently asked again, this time a little more kindly.

"No, marm," said the Texan, jerking his hitherto patient pony by the bridle till it performed feats of which an impartial observer could scarcely have suspected it.

"Don't reckon I could make Colfax before dark, do you?"

"Hardly," she said, turning away, "I'm much obliged to you, Mr. Jimson, for having taken this trouble—if the flat is on the other side, you need only call for it."

"Wall, good day, marm—I wish you luck," he added, with a touch of gallantry which her tears and sweet feminine presence had inspired. Then turning, he loped his horse rapidly forward, leaning well back in the saddle and his elbows sawing the air.

XIII

Melicent Hears the News

It was talked about and wept about at Place-du-Bois, that Grégoire should be dead. It seemed to them all so unbelievable. Yet, whatever hesitancy they had in accepting the fact of his death, was perforce removed by the convincing proof of Father O'Dowd's letter.

None could remember but sweetness and kindness of him. Even Nathan, who had been one day felled to earth by a crowbar in Grégoire's hand, had come himself to look at that deed as not altogether blamable in light of the provocation that had called it forth.

Fanny remembered those bouquets which had been daily offered to her forlornness at her arrival; and the conversations in which they had understood each other so well. The conviction that he was gone away beyond the possibility of knowing him further, moved her to tears. Hosmer, too, was grieved and shocked, without being able to view the event in the light of a calamity.

No one was left unmoved by the tidings which brought a lowering cloud even upon the brow of Aunt Belindy, to rest there the whole day. Deep were the mutterings she hurled at a fate that could have been so short-sighted as to remove from earth so bright an ornament as Grégoire. Her grief further spent much of itself upon the inoffensive Betsy, who, for some inscrutable reason was for twenty-four hours debarred entrance to the kitchen.

Thérèse seated at her desk, devoted a morning to the writing of letters, acquainting various members of the family with the unhappy intelligence. She wrote first to Madame Santien, living now her lazy life in Paris, with eyes closed to the duties that lay before her and heart choked up with an egoism that withered even the mother instincts. It was very difficult to withhold the reproach which she felt inclined to deal her; hard to refrain from upbraiding a selfishness which for a lifetime had appeared to Thérèse as criminal.

It was a matter less nice, less difficult, to write to the brothers—one up on the Red River plantation living as best he could; the other idling on the New Orleans streets. But it was after all a short and simple story to tell. There was no lingering illness to describe; no moment even of consciousness in which harrowing last words were to be gathered and recorded. Only a hot senseless quarrel to be told about; the speeding of a bullet with very sure aim, and—quick death.

Of course, masses must be said. Father O'Dowd was properly instructed. Père Antoine in Centerville was addressed on the subject. The Bishop of Natchitoches, respectfully asked to perform this last sad office for the departed soul. And the good old priest and friend at the New Orleans Cathedral, was informed of her desires. Not that Thérèse held very strongly to this saying of masses for the dead; but it had been a custom holding for generations in the family and which she was not disposed to abandon now, even if she had thought of it.

The last letter was sent to Melicent. Thérèse made it purposely short and pointed, with a bare statement of facts—a dry, unemotional telling, that sounded heartless when she read it over; but she let it go.

Melicent was standing in her small, quaint sitting-room, her back to the fire, and her hands clasped behind her. How handsome was this Melicent! Pouting now, and with eyes half covered by the dark shaded lids, as they gazed moodily out at the wild snowflakes that were hurrying like crazy things against the warm window pane and meeting their end there. A loose tea-gown clung in long folds about her. A dull colored thing, save for the two broad bands of sapphire plush hanging straight before, from throat to toe. Melicent was plainly dejected; not troubled, nor sad, only dejected, and very much bored; a condition that had made her yawn several times while she looked at the falling snow.

She was philosophizing a little. Wondering if the world this morning were really the unpleasant place that it appeared, or if these conditions of unpleasantness lay not rather within her own mental vision; a train of thought that might be supposed to have furnished her some degree of entertainment had she continued in its pursuit. But she chose rather to dwell on her causes of unhappiness, and thus convince herself that that unhappiness was indeed outside of her and around her and not by any possibility to be avoided or circumvented. There lay now a letter in her desk from David, filled with admonitions if not reproof which she felt to be not entirely unjust, on the disagreeable subject of Expenses. Looking around the pretty room she conceded to herself that here had been temptations which she could not reasonably have been expected to withstand. The temptation to lodge herself in this charming little flat; furnish it after her own liking; and install that delightful little old poverty-stricken English woman as keeper of Proprieties, with her irresistible white starched caps and her altogether delightful way of inquiring daily after that "poor, dear, kind Mr. Hosmer." It had all cost a little more than she had foreseen. But the worst of it, the very worst of it was, that she had already begun to ask herself if, for instance, it were not very irritating to see every day, that same branching palm, posing by the window, in that same yellow jardinière. If those draperies that confronted her were not becoming positively offensive in the monotony of their solemn folds. If the cuteness and quaintness of the poverty-stricken little English woman were not after all a source of entertainment that she would willingly forego on occasion. The answer to these questions was a sigh that ended in another yawn.

Then Melicent threw herself into a low easy chair by the table, took up her visiting book, and bending lazily with her arms resting on her knees, began to turn over its pages. The names which she saw there recalled to her mind an entertainment at which she had assisted on the previous afternoon. A progressive euchre party; and the remembrance of what she had there endured now filled her soul with horror.

She thought of those hundred cackling women—of course women are never cackling, it was Melicent's exaggerated way of expressing herself—packed into those small overheated rooms, around those twenty-five little tables; and how by no chance had she once found herself with a congenial set. And how that Mrs. Van Wycke had cheated! It was plain to Melicent that she had taken advantage of having fat Miss Bloomdale for a partner, who went to euchre parties only to show her hands and rings. And little Mrs. Brinke playing against her. Little Mrs. Brinke! A woman who only the other day had read an original paper entitled: "An Hour with Hegel" before her philosophy class; who had published that dry mystical affair "Light on the Inscrutable in Dante." How could such a one by any possibility be supposed to observe the disgusting action of Mrs. Van Wycke in throwing off on her partner's trump and swooping down on the last trick with her right bower? Melicent would have thought it beneath her to more than look her contempt as Mrs. Van Wycke rose with a triumphant laugh to take her place at a higher table, dragging the plastic Bloomdale with her. But she did mutter to herself now, "nasty thief."

"Johannah," Melicent called to her maid who sat sewing in the next room.

"Yes, Miss."

"You know Mrs. Van Wycke?"

"Mrs. Van Wycke, Miss? the lady with the pinted nose that I caught a-feeling of the curtains?"

"Yes, when she calls again I'm not at home. Do you understand? not at home."

"Yes, Miss."

It was gratifying enough to have thus summarily disposed of Mrs. Van Wycke; but it was a source of entertainment which was soon ended. Melicent continued to turn over the pages of her visiting book during which employment she came to the conclusion that these people whom she frequented were all very tiresome. All, all of them, except Miss Drake who had been absent in Europe for the past six months. Perhaps Mrs. Manning too, who was so seldom at home when Melicent called. Who when at home, usually rushed down with her bonnet on, breathless with "I can only spare you a moment, dear. It's very sweet of you to come." She was always just going to the "Home" where things had got into such a muddle whilst she was away for a week. Or it was that "Hospital" meeting where she thought certain members were secretly conniving at her removal from the presidency which she had held for so many years. She was always reading minutes at assemblages which Melicent knew nothing about; or introducing distinguished guests to Guild room meetings. Altogether Melicent saw very little of Mrs. Manning.

"Johannah, don't you hear the bell?"

"Yes, Miss," said Johannah, coming into the room and depositing a gown on which she had been working, on the back of a chair. "It's that postman," she said, as she fastened her needle to the bosom of her dress. "And such a one as he is, thinking that people must fly when he so much as touches the bell, and going off a writing of 'no answer to bell,' and me with my hand on the very door-knob."

"I notice that always happens when I'm out, Johannah; he's ringing again."

It was Thérèse's letter, and as Melicent turned it about and looked critically at the neatly written address, it was not without a hope that the reading of it might furnish her a moment's diversion. She did not faint. The letter did not "fall from her nerveless clasp." She rather held it very steadily. But she grew a shade paler and looked long into the fire. When she had read it three times she folded it slowly and carefully and locked it away in her desk.

"Johannah."

"Yes, Miss."

"Put that gown away; I shan't need it."

"Yes, Miss; and all the beautiful passmantry that you bought?"

"It makes no difference, I shan't use it. What's become of that black camel's-hair that Mrs. Gauche spoiled so last winter?"

"It's laid away, Miss, the same in the cedar chest as the day it came home from her hands and no more fit, that I'd be a shame meself and no claims to a dress-maker. And there's many a lady that she never would have seen a cent, let alone making herself pay for the spiling of it."

"Well, well, Johannah, never mind. Get it out, we'll see what can be done with it. I've had some painful news, and I shall wear mourning for a long, long time."

"Oh, Miss, it's not Mr. David! nor yet one of those sweet relations in Utica? leastways not I hope that beautiful Miss Gertrude, with such hair as I never see for the goldness of it and not dyed, except me cousin that's a nun, that her mother actually cried when it was cut off?"

"No, Johannah; only a very dear friend."

There were a few social engagements to be cancelled; and regrets to be sent out, which she attended to immediately. Then she turned again to look long into the fire. That crime for which she had scorned him, was wiped out now by expiation. For a long time—how long she could not yet determine—she would wrap herself in garb of mourning and move about in sorrowing—giving evasive answer to the curious who questioned her. Now might she live again through those summer months with Grégoire—those golden afternoons in the pine woods—whose aroma even now came back to her. She might look again into his loving brown eyes; feel beneath her touch the softness of his curls. She recalled a day when he had said, "Neva to see you—my God!" and how he had trembled. She recalled—strangely enough and for the first time—that one kiss, and a little tremor brought the hot color to her cheek.

Was she in love with Grégoire now that he was dead? Perhaps. At all events, for the next month, Melicent would not be bored.

XIV

A Step Too Far

Who of us has not known the presence of Misery? Perhaps as those fortunate ones whom he has but touched as he passed them by. It may be that we see but a promise of him as we look into the prophetic faces of children; into the eyes of those we love, and the awfulness of life's possibilities presses into our souls. Do we fly him? hearing him gain upon us panting close at our heels, till we turn from the desperation of uncertainty to grapple with him? In close scuffle we may vanquish him. Fleeing, we may elude him. But what if he creep into the sanctuary of our lives, with his subtle omnipresence, that we do not see in all its horror till we are disarmed; thrusting the burden of his companionship upon us to the end! However we turn he is there. However we shrink he is there. However we come or go, or sleep or wake he is before us. Till the keen sense grows dull with apathy at looking on him, and he becomes like the familiar presence of sin.

Into such callousness had Hosmer fallen. He had ceased to bruise his soul in restless endeavor of resistance. When the awful presence bore too closely upon him, he would close his eyes and brave himself to endurance. Yet Fate might have dealt him worse things.

But a man's misery is after all his own, to make of it what he will or what he can. And shall we be fools, wanting to lighten it with our platitudes?

My friend, your trouble I know weighs. That you should be driven by earthly needs to drag the pinioned spirit of your days through rut and mire. But think of the millions who are doing the like. Or is it your boy, that part of your own self and that other dearer self, who is walking in evil ways? Why, I know a man whose son was hanged the other day; hanged on the gibbet; think of it. If you be quivering while the surgeon cuts away that right arm, remember the poor devil in the hospital yesterday who had both his sawed off.

Oh, have done, with your mutilated men and your sons on gibbets! What are they to me? My hurt is greater than all, because it is my own. If it be only that day after day I must look with warm entreaty into eyes that are cold. Let it be but that peculiar trick of feature which I have come to hate, seen each morning across the breakfast table. That recurrent pin-prick: it hurts. The blow that lays the heart in twain: it kills. Let be mine which will; it is the one that counts.

If Misery kill a man, that ends it. But Misery seldom deals so summarily with his victims. And while they are spared to earth, we find them usually sustaining life after the accepted fashion.

Hosmer was seated at table, having finished his breakfast. He had also finished glancing over the contents of a small memorandum book, which he replaced in his pocket. He then looked at his wife sitting opposite him, but turned rather hastily to gaze with a certain entreaty into the big kind eyes of the great shaggy dog who stood—the shameless beggar—at his side.

"I knew there was something wrong," he said abruptly, with his eyes still fixed on the dog, and his fingers thrust into the animal's matted wool, "Where's the mail this morning?"

"I don't know if that stupid boy's gone for it or not. I told him. You can't depend on any one in a place like this."

Fanny had scarcely touched the breakfast before her, and now pushed aside her cup still half filled with coffee.

"Why, how's that? Sampson seems to do the right thing."

"Yes, Sampson; but he ain't here. That boy of Minervy's been doing his work all morning."

Minervy's boy was even now making his appearance, carrying a good sized bundle of papers and letters, with which he walked boldly up to Hosmer, plainly impressed with the importance of this new rôle.

"Well, colonel; so you've taken Sampson's place?" Hosmer observed, receiving the mail from the boy's little black paws.

"My name's Major, suh. Maje; dats my name. I ain't tuck Sampson's place: no, suh."

"Oh, he's having a day off—" Hosmer went on, smiling quizzingly at the dapper little darkey, and handing him a red apple from the dish of fruit standing in the center of the table. Maje received it with a very unmilitary bob of acknowledgment.

"He yonda home 'cross de riva, suh. He ben too late fu' kotch de flat's mornin' An' he holla an' holla. He know dey warn't gwine cross dat flat 'gin jis' fu' Sampson."

Hosmer had commenced to open his letters. Fanny with her elbows on the table, asked the boy—with a certain uneasiness in her voice—

"Ain't he coming at all to-day? Don't he know all the work he's got to do? His mother ought to make him."

"Don't reckon. Dat away Sampson: he git mad he stay mad," with which assurance Maje vanished through the rear door, towards the region of the kitchen, to seek more substantial condiments than the apple which he still clutched firmly.

One of the letters was for Fanny, which her husband handed her. When he had finished reading his own, he seemed disposed to linger, for he took from the fruit dish the mate to the red apple he had given Maje, and commenced to peel it with his clasp knife.

"What has our friend Belle Worthington to say for herself?" he inquired good humoredly. "How does she get on with those Creoles down there?"

"You know as well as I do, Belle Worthington ain't going to mix with Creoles. She can't talk French if she wanted to. She says Muddy-Graw don't begin to compare with the Veiled Prophets. It's just what I thought—with their 'Muddy-Graw,'" Fanny added, contemptuously.

"Coming from such high authority, we'll consider that verdict a final clincher," Hosmer laughed a little provokingly.

Fanny was looking again through the several sheets of Belle Worthington's letter. "She says if I'll agree to go back with her, she'll pass this way again."

"Well, why don't you? A little change wouldn't hurt."

"'Tain't because I want to stay here, Lord knows. A God-forsaken place like this. I guess you'd be glad enough," she added, with voice shaking a little at her own boldness.

He closed his knife, placed it in his pocket, and looked at his wife, completely puzzled.

The power of speech had come to her, for she went on, in an unnatural tone, however, and fumbling nervously with the dishes before her. "I'm fool enough about some things, but I ain't quite such a fool as that."

"What are you talking about, Fanny?"

"That woman wouldn't ask anything better than for me to go to St. Louis."

Hosmer was utterly amazed. He leaned his arms on the table, clasping his hands together and looked at his wife.

"That woman? Belle Worthington? What *do* you mean, any way?"

"I don't mean Belle Worthington," she said excitedly, with two deep red spots in her cheeks. "I'm talking about Mrs. Laferm."

He thrust his hand into his pockets and leaned back in his chair. No amazement now, but very pale, and with terrible concentration of glance.

"Well, then, don't talk about Mrs. Lafirme," he said very slowly, not taking his eyes from her face.

"I will talk about her, too. She ain't worth talking about," she blurted incoherently. "It's time for somebody to talk about a woman passing herself off for a saint, and trying to take other women's husbands—"

"Shut up!" cried Hosmer maddened with sudden fury, and rising violently from his chair.

"I won't shut up," Fanny cried excitedly back at him; rising also. "And what's more I won't stay here and have you making love under my very eyes to a woman that's no better than she ought to be."

She meant to say more, but Hosmer grasped her arm with such a grasp, that had it been her throat she would never have spoken more. The other hand went to his pocket, with fingers clutching the clasp knife there.

"By heaven—I'll—kill you!" every word weighted with murder, panted close in her terrified face. What she would have uttered died upon her pale lips, when her frightened eyes beheld the usually calm face of her husband distorted by a passion of which she had not dreamed.

"David," she faltered, "let go my arm."

Her voice broke the spell that held him, and brought him again to his senses. His fingers slowly relaxed their tense hold. A sigh that was something between a moan and a gasp came with his deliverance and shook him. All the horror now was in his own face as he seized his hat and hurried speechless away.

Fanny remained for a little while dazed. Hers was not the fine nature that would stay cruelly stunned after such a scene. Her immediate terror being past, the strongest resultant emotion was one of self-satisfaction at having spoken out her mind.

But there was a stronger feeling yet, moving and possessing her; crowding out every other. A pressing want that only Sampson's coming would relieve, and which bade fair to drive her to any extremity if it were not appeased.

XV

A Fateful Solution

Hosmer passed the day with a great pain at his heart. His hasty and violent passion of the morning had added another weight for his spirit to drag about, and which he could not cast off. No feeling of resentment remained with him; only wonder at his wife's misshapen knowledge and keen self-rebuke of his own momentary forgetfulness. Even knowing Fanny as he did, he could not rid himself of the haunting dread of having wounded her nature cruelly. He felt much as a man who in a moment of anger inflicts an irreparable hurt upon some small, weak, irresponsible creature, and must bear regret for his madness. The only reparation that lay within his power—true, one that seemed inadequate—was an open and manly apology and confession of wrong. He would feel better when it was made. He would perhaps find relief in discovering that the wound he had inflicted was not so deep—so dangerous as he feared.

With such end in view he came home early in the afternoon. His wife was not there. The house was deserted. Even the servants had disappeared. It took but a moment for him to search the various rooms and find them one after the other, unoccupied. He went out on the porch and looked around. The raw air chilled him. The wind was blowing violently, bringing dashes of rain along with it from massed clouds that hung leaden between sky and earth. Could she have gone over to the house? It was unlikely, for he knew her to have avoided Mrs. Lafirme of late, with a persistence that had puzzled him to seek its cause, which had only fully revealed itself in the morning Yet, where else could she be? An undefined terror was laying hold of him. His sensitive nature, in exaggerating its own heartlessness, was blindly overestimating the delicacy of hers. To what may he not have driven her? What hitherto untouched chord may he not have started into painful quivering? Was it for him to gauge the endurance of a woman's spirit? Fanny was not now the wife whom he hated; his own act of the morning had changed her into the human being, the weak creature whom he had wronged.

In quitting the house she must have gone unprepared for the inclement weather, for there hung her heavy wrap in its accustomed place, with her umbrella beside it. He seized both and buttoning his own great coat about him, hurried away and over to Mrs. Lafirme's. He found that lady in the sitting-room.

"Isn't Fanny here?" he asked abruptly, with no word of greeting.

"No," she answered looking up at him, and seeing the evident uneasiness in his face. "Isn't she at home? Is anything wrong?"

"Oh, everything is wrong," he returned desperately, "But the immediate wrong is that she has disappeared—I must find her."

Thérèse arose at once and called to Betsy who was occupied on the front veranda.

"Yas, um," the girl answered to her mistress' enquiry. "I seed ma'am Hosma goin' to'ads de riva good hour 'go. She mus' crost w'en Nathan tuck dat load ova. I yain't seed 'er comin' back yit."

Hosmer left the house hastily, hardly reassured by Betsy's information. Thérèse's glance—speculating and uneasy—followed his hurrying figure till it disappeared from sight.

The crossing was an affair of extreme difficulty, and which Nathan was reluctant to undertake until he should have gathered a "load" that would justify him in making it. In his estimation, Hosmer did not meet such requirement, even taken in company with the solitary individual who had been sitting on his horse with Egyptian patience for long unheeded moments, the rain beating down upon his back, while he waited the ferryman's pleasure. But Nathan's determination was not proof against the substantial inducements which Hosmer held out to him; and soon they were launched, all hands assisting in the toilsome passage.

The water, in rising to an unaccustomed height, had taken on an added and tremendous swiftness. The red turbid stream was eddying and bulging and hurrying with terrific swiftness between its shallow banks, striking with an immensity of power against the projection of land on which stood Marie Louise's cabin, and rebounding in great circling waves that spread and lost themselves in the seething turmoil. The cable used in crossing the unwieldly flat had long been submerged and the posts which held it wrenched from their fastenings. The three men, each with his long heavy oar in hand began to pull up stream, using a force that brought the swelling veins like iron tracings upon their foreheads where the sweat had gathered as if the day were midsummer. They made their toilsome way by slow inches, that finally landed them breathless and exhausted on the opposite side.

What could have been the inducement to call Fanny out on such a day and such a venture? The answer came only too readily from Hosmer's reproaching conscience. And now, where to seek her? There was nothing to guide him; to indicate the course she might have taken. The rain was falling heavily and in gusts and through it he looked about at the small cabins standing dreary in their dismantled fields. Marie Louise's was the nearest at hand and towards it he directed his steps.

The big good-natured negress had seen his approach from the window, for she opened the door to him before he had time to knock, and entering he saw Fanny seated before the fire holding a pair of very wet smoking feet to dry. His first sensation was one of relief at finding her safe and housed. His next, one of uncertainty as to the kind and degree of resentment which he felt confident must now show itself. But this last was soon dispelled, for turning, she greeted him with a laugh. He would have rather a blow. That laugh said so many things—too many things. True, it removed the dread which had been haunting him all day, but it shattered what seemed to have been now his last illusion regarding this woman. That unsounded chord which he feared he had touched was after all but one in harmony with the rest of her common nature. He saw too at a glance that her dominant passion had been leading and now controlled her. And by one of those rapid trains of thought in which odd and detached fancies, facts, impressions and observations form themselves into an orderly sequence leading to a final conviction—all was made plain to him that before had puzzled him. She need not have told him her reason for crossing the river, he knew it. He dismissed at once the attitude with which he had thought to approach her. Here was no forgiveness to be asked of dulled senses. No bending in expiation of faults committed. He was here as master.

"Fanny, what does this mean?" he asked in cold anger; with no heat now, no passion.

"Yaas, me tell madame, she goin' fur ketch cole si she don' mine out. Dat not fur play dat kine wedder, no. Teck chair, M'sieur; dry you'se'f leet beet. Me mek you one cup coffee."

Hosmer declined the good Marie Louise's kind proffer of coffee, but he seated himself and waited for Fanny to speak.

"You know if you want a thing done in this place, you've got to do it yourself. I've heard you say it myself, time and time again about those people at the mill," she said.

"Could it have been so urgent as to call you out on a day like this, and with such a perilous crossing? Couldn't you have found some one else to come for you?"

"Who? I'd like to know. Just tell me who? It's nothing to you if we're without servants, but I'm not going to stand it. I ain't going to let Sampson act like that without knowing what he means," said Fanny sharply.

"Dat Sampson, he one leet dev'," proffered Marie Louise, with laudable design of shifting blame upon the easy shoulders of Sampson, in event of the domestic jar which she anticipated. "No use try do nuttin' 'id Sampson, M'sieur."

"I had to know something, one way or the other," Fanny said in a tone which carried apology, rather by courtesy than by what she considered due.

Hosmer walked to the window where he looked out upon the dreary, desolate scene, little calculated to cheer him. The river was just below; and from this window he could gaze down upon the rushing current as it swept around the bend further up and came striking against this projection with a force all its own. The rain was falling still; steadily, blindingly, with wild clatter against the shingled roof so close above their heads. It coursed in little swift rivulets down the furrows of the almost perpendicular banks. It mingled in a demon dance with the dull, red water. There was something inviting to Hosmer in the scene. He wanted to be outside there making a part of it. He wanted to feel that rain and wind beating upon him. Within, it was stifling, maddening; with his wife's presence there, charging the room with an atmosphere of hate that was possessing him and beginning to course through his veins as it had never done before.

"Do you want to go home?" he asked bluntly, turning half around.

"You must be crazy," she replied, with a slow, upward glance out the window, then down at her feet that were still poised on the low stool that Marie Louise had placed for her.

"You'd better come." He could not have said what moved him, unless it were recklessness and defiance.

"I guess you're dreaming, or something, David. You go on home if you want. Nobody asked you to come after me any way. I'm able to take care of myself, I guess. Ain't you going to take the umbrella?" she added, seeing him start for the door empty handed.

"Oh, it doesn't matter about the rain," he answered without a look back as he went out and slammed the door after him.

"M'sieur look lak he not please," said Marie Louise, with plain regret at the turn of affairs. "You see he no lak you go out in dat kine wedder, me know dat."

"Oh, bother," was Fanny's careless reply. "This suits me well enough; I don't care how long it lasts."

She was in Marie Louise's big rocker, balancing comfortably back and forth with a swing that had become automatic. She felt "good," as she would have termed it herself; her visit to Sampson's hut having not been without results tending to that condition. The warmth of the room was very agreeable in contrast to the bleakness of out-doors. She felt free and moved to exercise a looseness of tongue with the amiable old negress which was not common with her. The occurrences of the morning were gradually withdrawing themselves into a distant perspective that left her in the attitude of a spectator rather than that of an actor. And she laughed and talked with Marie Louise, and rocked, and rocked herself on into drowsiness.

Hosmer had no intention of returning home without his wife. He only wanted to be out under the sky; he wanted to breathe, to use his muscles again. He would go and help cross the flat if need be; an occupation that promised him relief in physical effort. He joined Nathan, whom he found standing under a big live-oak, disputing with an old colored woman who wanted to cross to get back to her family before supper time.

"You didn' have no call to come ova in de fus' place," he was saying to her, "you womens is alluz runnin' back'ards and for'ards like skeard rabbit in de co'n fiel'."

"I don' stan' no sich talk is dat f'om you. Ef you kiant tin' to yo' business o' totin' folks w'en dey wants, you betta quit. You done cheat Mose out o' de job, anyways; we all knows dat."

"Mine out, woman, you gwine git hu't. Jis' le'me see Mose han'le dat 'ar flat onct: Jis' le'me. He lan' you down to de Mouf' fo' you knows it."

"Let me tell you, Nathan," said Hosmer, looking at his watch, "say you wait a quarter of an hour and if no one else comes, we'll cross Aunt Agnes anyway."

"Dat 'nudda t'ing ef you wants to go back, suh."

Aunt Agnes was grumbling now at Hosmer's proposal that promised to keep her another quarter of an hour from her expectant family, when a big lumbering creaking wagon drove up, with its load of baled cotton all covered with tarpaulins.

"Dah!" exclaimed Nathan at sight of the wagon, "ef I'd 'a listened to yo' jawin'—what?"

"Ef you'd listen to me, you'd 'tin' to yo' business betta 'an you does," replied Aunt Agnes, raising a very battered umbrella over her grotesquely apparelled figure, as she stepped from under the shelter of the tree to take her place in the flat.

But she still met with obstacles, for the wagon must needs go first. When it had rolled heavily into place with much loud and needless swearing on the part of the driver who, being a white man, considered Hosmer's presence no hindrance, they let go the chain, and once again pulled out. The crossing was even more difficult now, owing to the extra weight of the wagon.

"I guess you earn your money, Nathan," said Hosmer bending and quivering with the efforts he put forth.

"Yas, suh, I does; an' dis job's wuf mo' 'an I gits fu' it."

"All de same you done lef' off wurking crap sence you start it," mumbled Aunt Agnes.

"You gwine git hu't, woman; I done tole you dat; don' wan' listen," returned Nathan with halting breath.

"Who gwine hu't me?"

Whether from tardy gallantry or from pre-occupation with his arduous work, Nathan offered no reply to this challenge, and his silence left Aunt Agnes in possession of the field.

They were in full mid-stream. Hosmer and the teamster were in the fore end of the boat; Nathan in the rear, and Aunt Agnes standing in the center between the wagon and the protecting railing, against which she leaned her clasped hands that still upheld the semblance of umbrella.

The ill-mated horses stood motionless, letting fall their dejected heads with apathetic droop. The rain was dripping from their glistening coats, and making a great patter as it fell upon the tarpaulins covering the cotton bales.

Suddenly came an exclamation: "Gret God!" from Aunt Agnes, so genuine in its amazement and dismay, that the three men with one accord looked quickly up at her, then at the point on which her terrified gaze was fixed. Almost on the instant of the woman's cry, was heard a shrill, piercing, feminine scream.

What they saw was the section of land on which stood Marie Louise's cabin, undermined—broken away from the main body and gradually gliding into the water. It must have sunk with a first abrupt wrench, for the brick chimney was shaken from its foundation, the smoke issuing in dense clouds from its shattered sides, the house toppling and the roof caving. For a moment Hosmer lost his senses. He could but look, as if at some awful apparition that must soon pass from sight and leave him again in possession of his reason. The leaning house was half submerged when Fanny appeared at the door, like a figure in a dream; seeming a natural part of the awfulness of it. He only gazed on. The two negroes uttered loud lamentations.

"Pull with the current!" cried the teamster, first to regain his presence of mind. It had needed but this, to awaken Hosmer to the situation.

"Leave off," he cried at Nathan, who was wringing his hands. "Take hold that oar or I'll throw you overboard." The trembling ashen negro obeyed on the instant.

"Hold fast—for God's sake—hold fast!" he shouted to Fanny, who was clinging with swaying figure to the door post. Of Marie Louise there was no sign.

The caved bank now remained fixed; but Hosmer knew that at any instant it was liable to disappear before his riveted gaze.

How heavy the flat was! And the horses had caught the contagion of terror and were plunging madly.

"Whip those horses and their load into the river," called Hosmer, "we've got to lighten at any price."

"Them horses an' cotton's worth money," interposed the alarmed teamster.

"Force them into the river, I say; I'll pay you twice their value."

"You 'low to pay fur the cotton, too?"

"Into the river with them or I'll brain you!" he cried, maddened at the weight and delay that were holding them back.

The frightened animals seemed to ask nothing more than to plunge into the troubled water; dragging their load with them.

They were speeding rapidly towards the scene of catastrophe; but to Hosmer they crawled—the moments were hours. "Hold on! hold fast!" he called again and again to his wife. But even as he cried out, the detached section of earth swayed, lurched to one side—plunged to the other, and the whole mass was submerged—leaving the water above it in wild agitation.

A cry of horror went up from the spectators—all but Hosmer. He cast aside his oar—threw off his coat and hat; worked an instant without avail at his wet clinging boots, and with a leap was in the water, swimming towards the spot where the cabin had gone down. The current bore him on without much effort of his own. The flat was close up with him; but he could think of it no longer as a means of rescue. Detached pieces of timber from the ruined house were beginning to rise to the surface. Then something floating softly on the water: a woman's dress, but too far for him to reach it.

When Fanny appeared again, Hosmer was close beside her. His left arm was quickly thrown about her. She was insensible, and he remembered that it was best so, for had she been in possession of her reason, she might have struggled and impeded his movements. He held her fast—close to him and turned to regain the shore. Another horrified shriek went up from the occupants of the flat-boat not far away, and Hosmer knew no more—for a great plunging beam struck him full upon the forehead.

When consciousness came back to him, he found that he lay extended in the flat, which was fastened to the shore. The confused sound of many voices mingled with a ringing din that filled his ears. A warm stream was trickling down over his cheek. Another body lay beside him. Now they were lifting him. Thérèse's face was somewhere— very near, he saw it dimly and that it was white—and he fell again into insensibility.

XVI

To Him Who Waits

The air was filled with the spring and all its promises. Full with the sound of it, the smell of it, the deliciousness of it. Such sweet air; soft and strong, like the touch of a brave woman's hand. The air of an early March day in New Orleans. It was folly to shut it out from nook or cranny. Worse than folly the lady thought who was making futile endeavors to open the car window near which she sat. Her face had grown pink with the effort. She had bit firmly into her red nether lip, making it all the redder; and then sat down from the unaccomplished feat to look ruefully at the smirched finger tips of her Parisian gloves. This flavor of Paris was well about her; in the folds of her graceful wrap that set to her fine shoulders. It was plainly a part of the little black velvet toque that rested on her blonde hair. Even the umbrella and one small valise which she had just laid on the seat opposite her, had Paris written plain upon them.

These were impressions which the little grey-garbed conventional figure, some seats removed, had been noting since the striking lady had entered the car. Points likely to have escaped a man, who—unless a minutely observant one,—would only have seen that she was handsome and worthy of an admiration that he might easily fancy rising to devotion.

Beside herself and the little grey-garbed figure was an interesting family group at the far end of the car. A husband, but doubly a father, surrounded and sat upon by a small band of offspring. A wife— presumably a mother—absorbed with the view of the outside world and the elaborate gold chain that hung around her neck.

The presence of a large valise, an overcoat, a cane and an umbrella disposed on another seat, bespoke a further occupant, likely to be at present in the smoking car.

The train pushed out from the depôt. The porter finally made tardy haste to the assistance of the lady who had been attempting to open the window, and when the fresh morning air came blowing in upon her Thérèse leaned back in her seat with a sigh of content.

There was a full day's journey before her. She would not reach Place-du-Bois before dark, but she did not shrink from those hours that were to be passed alone. She rather welcomed the quiet of them after a visit to New Orleans full of pleasant disturbances. She was eager to be home again. She loved Place-du-Bois with a love that was real; that had grown deep since it was the one place in the world which she could connect with the presence of David Hosmer. She had often wondered— indeed was wondering now—if the memory of those happenings to which he belonged would ever grow strange and far away to her. It was a trick of memory with which she indulged herself on occasion, this one of retrospection. Beginning with that June day when she had sat in the hall and watched the course of a white sunshade over the tops of the bending corn.

Such idle thoughts they were with their mingling of bitter and sweet—leading nowhere. But she clung to them and held to them as if to a refuge which she might again and again return to.

The picture of that one terrible day of Fanny's death, stood out in sharp prominent lines; a touch of the old agony always coming back as she remembered how she had believed Hosmer dead too—lying so pale and bleeding before her. Then the parting which had held not so much of sorrow as of awe and bewilderment in it: when sick, wounded and broken he had gone away at once with the dead body of his wife; when the two had clasped hands without words that dared be uttered.

But that was a year ago. And Thérèse thought many things might come about in a year. Anyhow, might not such length of time be hoped to rub the edge off a pain that was not by its nature lasting?

That time of acute trouble seemed to have thrown Hosmer back upon his old diffidence. The letter he wrote her after a painful illness which prostrated him on his arrival in St. Louis, was stiff and formal, as men's letters are apt to be, though it had breathed an untold story of loyalty which she had felt at the time, and still cherished. Other letters—a few—had gone back and forth between them, till Hosmer had gone away to the sea-shore with Melicent, to recuperate, and June coming, Thérèse had sailed from New Orleans for Paris, whither she had passed six months.

Things had not gone well at Place-du-Bois during her absence, the impecunious old kinsman whom she had left in charge, having a decided preference for hunting the *Gros-Bec* and catching trout in the lake to supervising the methods of a troublesome body of blacks. So Thérèse had had much to engage her thoughts from the morbid channel into which those of a more idle woman might have drifted.

She went occasionally enough to the mill. There at least she was always sure to hear Hosmer's name—and what a charm the sound of it had for her. And what a delight it was to her eyes when she caught sight of an envelope lying somewhere on desk or table of the office, addressed in his handwriting. That was a weakness which she could not pardon herself; but which staid with her, seeing that the same trifling cause never failed to awaken the same unmeasured delight. She had even trumped up an excuse one day for carrying off one of Hosmer's business letters—indeed of the dryest in substance, and which, when half-way home, she had torn into the smallest bits and scattered to the winds, so overcome was she by a sense of her own absurdity.

Thérèse had undergone the ordeal of having her ticket scrutinized, commented upon and properly punched by the suave conductor. The little conventional figure had given over the contemplation of Parisian styles and betaken herself to the absorbing pages of a novel which she read through smoked glasses. The husband and father had peeled and distributed his second outlay of bananas amongst his family. It was at this moment that Thérèse, looking towards the door, saw Hosmer enter the car.

She must have felt his presence somewhere near; his being there and coming towards her was so much a part of her thoughts. She held out her hand to him and made place beside her, as if he had left her but a half hour before. All the astonishment was his. But he pressed her hand and took the seat she offered him.

"You knew I was on the train?" he asked.

"Oh, no, how should I?"

Then naturally followed question and answer.

Yes, he was going to Place-du-Bois.

No, the mill did not require his presence; it had been very well managed during his absence.

Yes, she had been to New Orleans. Had had a very agreeable visit. Beautiful weather for city dwellers. But such dryness. So disastrous to the planters.

Yes—quite likely there would be rain next month: there usually was in April. But indeed there was need of more than April showers for that stiff land—that strip along the bayou, if he remembered? Oh, he remembered quite well, but for all that he did not know what she was talking about. She did not know herself. Then they grew silent; not from any feeling of the absurdity of such speech between them, for each had but listened to the other's voice. They became silently absorbed by the consciousness of each other's nearness. She was looking at his hand that rested on his knee, and thinking it fuller than she remembered it before. She was aware of some change in him which she had not the opportunity to define; but this firmness and fullness of the hand was part of it. She looked up into his face then, to find the same change there, together with a new content. But what she noted beside was the dull scar on his forehead, coming out like a red letter when his eyes looked into her own. The sight of it was like a hurt. She had forgotten it might be there, telling its story of pain through the rest of his life.

"Thérèse," Hosmer said finally, "won't you look at me?"

She was looking from the window. She did not turn her head, but her hand went out and met his that was on the seat close beside her. He held it firmly; but soon with an impatient movement drew down the loose wristlet of her glove and clasped his fingers around her warm wrist.

"Thérèse," he said again; but more unsteadily, "look at me."

"Not here," she answered him, "not now, I mean." And presently she drew her hand away from him and held it for a moment pressed firmly over her eyes. Then she looked at him with brave loving glance.

"It's been so long," she said, with the suspicion of a sigh.

"Too long," he returned, "I couldn't have borne it but for you—the thought of you always present with me; helping me to take myself out of the past. That was why I waited—till I could come to you free. Have you an idea, I wonder, how you have been a promise, and can be the fulfillment of every good that life may give to a man?"

"No, I don't know," she said a little hopelessly, taking his hand again, "I have seen myself at fault in following what seemed the only right. I feel as if there were no way to turn for the truth. Old supports appear to be giving way beneath me. They were so secure before. It commenced, you remember—oh, you know when it must have begun. But do you think, David, that it's right we should find our happiness out of that past of pain and sin and trouble?"

"Thérèse," said Hosmer firmly, "the truth in its entirety isn't given to man to know—such knowledge, no doubt, would be beyond human endurance. But we make a step towards it, when we learn that there is rottenness and evil in the world, masquerading as right and morality—when we learn to know the living spirit from the dead letter. I have not cared to stop in this struggle of life to question. You, perhaps, wouldn't dare to alone. Together, dear one, we will work it out. Be sure there is a way—we may not find it in the end, but we will at least have tried."

XVII

Conclusion

One month after their meeting on the train, Hosmer and Thérèse had gone together to Centerville where they had been made one, as the saying goes, by the good Père Antoine; and without more ado, had driven back to Place-du-Bois: Mr. and Mrs. Hosmer. The event had caused more than the proverbial nine days' talk. Indeed, now, two months after, it was still the absorbing theme that occupied the dwellers of the parish: and such it promised to remain till supplanted by something of sufficient dignity and importance to usurp its place.

But of the opinions, favorable and other, that were being exchanged regarding them and their marriage, Hosmer and Thérèse heard little and would have cared less, so absorbed were they in the overmastering happiness that was holding them in thralldom. They could not yet bring themselves to look at it calmly—this happiness. Even the intoxication of it seemed a thing that promised to hold. Through love they had sought each other, and now the fulfillment of that love had brought more than tenfold its promise to both. It was a royal love; a generous love and a rich one in its revelation. It was a magician that had touched life for them and changed it into a glory. In giving them to each other, it was moving them to the fullness of their own capabilities. Much to do in two little months; but what cannot love do?

"Could it give a woman more than this?" Thérèse was saying softly to herself. Her hands were clasped as in prayer and pressed together against her bosom. Her head bowed and her lips touching the intertwined fingers. She spoke of her own emotion; of a certain sweet turmoil that was stirring within her, as she stood out in the soft June twilight waiting for her husband to come. Waiting to hear the new ring in his voice that was like a song of joy. Waiting to see that new strength and courage in his face, of whose significance she lost nothing. To see the new light that had come in his eyes with happiness. All gifts which love had given her.

"Well, at last," she said, going to the top of the steps to meet him when he came. Her welcome was in her eyes.

"At last," he echoed, with a sigh of relief; pressing her hand which she held out to him and raising it to his lips.

He did not let it go, but passed it through his arm, and together they turned to walk up and down the veranda.

"You didn't expect me at noon, did you?" he asked, looking down at her.

"No; you said you'd be likely not to come; but I hoped for you all the same. I thought you'd manage it some way."

"No," he answered her, laughing, "my efforts failed. I used even strategy. Held out the temptation of your delightful Creole dishes and all that. Nothing was of any avail. They were all business and I had to be all business too, the whole day long. It was horribly stupid."

She pressed his arm significantly.

"And do you think they will put all that money into the mill, David? Into the business?"

"No doubt of it, dear. But they're shrewd fellows: didn't commit themselves in any way. Yet I could see they were impressed. We rode for hours through the woods this morning and they didn't leave a stick of timber unscrutinized. We were out on the lake, too, and they were like ferrets into every cranny of the mill."

"But won't that give you more to do?"

"No, it will give me less: division of labor, don't you see? It will give me more time to be with you."

"And to help with the plantation," his wife suggested.

"No, no, Madame Thérèse," he laughed, "I'll not rob you of your occupation. I'll put no bungling hand into your concerns. I know a sound piece of timber when I see it; but I should hardly be able to tell a sample of Sea Island cotton from the veriest low middling."

"Oh, that's absurd, David. Do you know you're getting to talk such nonsense since we're married; you remind me sometimes of Melicent."

"Of Melicent? Heaven forbid! Why, I have a letter from her," he said, feeling in his breast pocket. "The size and substance of it have actually weighted my pocket the whole day."

"Melicent talking weighty things? That's something new," said Thérèse interested.

"Is Melicent ever anything else than new?" he enquired.

They went and sat together on the bench at the corner of the veranda, where the fading Western light came over their shoulders. A quizzical smile came into his eyes as he unfolded his sister's letter—with Thérèse still holding his arm and sitting very close to him.

"Well," he said, glancing over the first few pages—his wife following—"she's given up her charming little flat and her quaint little English woman: concludes I was right about the expense, etc., etc. But here comes the gist of the matter," he said, reading from the letter—"'I know you won't object to the trip, David, I have my heart so set on it. The expense will be trifling, seeing there are four of us to divide carriage hire, restaurant and all that: and it counts.

"'If you only knew Mrs. Griesmann I'd feel confident of your consent. You'd be perfectly fascinated with her. She's one of those highly gifted women who knows everything. She's very much interested in me. Thinks to have found that I have a quick comprehensive intellectualism (she calls it) that has been misdirected. I think there is something in that, David; you know yourself I never did care really for society. She says it's impossible to ever come to a true knowledge of life as it is—which should be every one's aim—without studying certain fundamental truths and things.'"

"Oh," breathed Thérèse, overawed.

"But wait—but listen," said Hosmer, "'Natural History and all that—and we're going to take that magnificent trip through the West—the Yosemite and so forth. It appears the flora of California is especially interesting and we're to carry those delicious little tin boxes strapped over our shoulders to hold specimens. Her son and daughter are both, in their way, striking. He isn't handsome; rather the contrary; but so serene and collected—so intensely bitter—his mother tells me he's a pessimist. And the daughter really puts me to shame, child as she is, with the amount of her knowledge. She labels all her mother's specimens in Latin. Oh, I feel there's so much to be learned. Mrs. Griesmann thinks I ought to wear glasses during the trip. Says we often require them without knowing it ourselves—that they are so restful. She has some theory about it. I'm trying a pair, and see a great deal better through them than I expected to. Only they don't hold on very well, especially when I laugh.

"'Who do you suppose seized on to me in Vandervoort's the other day, but that impertinent Mrs. Belle Worthington! Positively took me by the coat and commenced to gush about dear sister Thérèse. She said: "I tell you what, my dear—" called me my dear at the highest pitch, and that odious Mrs. Van Wycke behind us listening and pretending to examine a lace handkerchief. "That Mrs. Lafirme's a trump," she said—"too good for most any man. Hope you won't take offense, but I must say, your brother David's a perfect stick—it's what I always said." Can you conceive of such shocking impertinence?'

"Well; Belle Worthington does possess the virtue of candor," said Hosmer amused and folding the letter. "That's about all there is, except a piece of scandal concerning people you don't know; that wouldn't interest you."

"But it would interest me," Thérèse insisted, with a little wifely resentment that her husband should have a knowledge of people that excluded her.

"Then you shall hear it," he said, turning to the letter again. "Let's see—'conceive—shocking impertinence—' oh, here it is.

"'Don't know if you have learned the horrible scandal; too dreadful to talk about. I shall send you the paper. I always knew that Lou Dawson was a perfidious creature—and Bert Rodney! You never did like him, David; but he was always so much the gentleman in his manners—you must admit that. Who could have dreamed it of him. Poor Mrs. Rodney is after all the one to be pitied. She is utterly prostrated. Refuses to see even her most intimate friends. It all came of those two vile wretches thinking Jack Dawson out of town when he wasn't; for he was right there following them around in their perambulations. And the outcome is that Mr. Rodney has his beauty spoiled they say forever; the shot came very near being fatal. But poor, poor Mrs. Rodney!

"'Well, good-bye, you dearest David mine. How I wish you both knew Mrs. Griesmann. Give that sweet sister Thérèse as many kisses as she will stand for me.

MELICENT

This time Hosmer put the letter into his pocket, and Thérèse asked with a little puzzled air: "What do you suppose is going to become of Melicent, anyway, David?"

"I don't know, love, unless she marries my friend Homeyer."

"Now, David, you are trying to mystify me. I believe there's a streak of perversity in you after all."

"Of course there is; and here comes Mandy to say that 'suppa's gittin' cole.'"

"Aunt B'lindy 'low suppa on de table gittin' cole," said Mandy, retreating at once from the fire of their merriment.

Thérèse arose and held her two hands out to her husband.

He took them but did not rise; only leaned further back on the seat and looked up at her.

"Oh, supper's a bore; don't you think so?" he asked.

"No, I don't," she replied. "I'm hungry, and so are you. Come, David."

"But look, Thérèse, just when the moon has climbed over the top of that live-oak? We can't go now. And then Melicent's request; we must think about that."

"Oh, surely not, David," she said, drawing back.

"Then let me tell you something," and he drew her head down and whispered something in her pink ear that he just brushed with his lips. It made Thérèse laugh and turn very rosy in the moonlight.

Can that be Hosmer? Is this Thérèse? Fie, fie. It is time we were leaving them.

A Note About the Author

Kate Chopin (1850–1904) was an American writer. Born in St. Louis, Missouri to a family with French and Irish ancestry, Chopin was raised Roman Catholic. An avid reader, Chopin graduated from Sacred Heart Convent in 1968 before marrying Oscar Chopin, with whom she moved to New Orleans in 1870. The two had six children before Oscar's death in 1882, which left the family with extensive debts and forced Kate to take over her husband's businesses, including the management of several plantations and a general store. In the early 1890s, back in St. Louis and suffering from depression, Chopin began writing short stories, articles, and translations for local newspapers and literary magazines. Although she achieved moderate critical acclaim for her second novel, *The Awakening* (1899)—now considered a classic of American literature and a pioneering work of feminist fiction—fame and success eluded her in her lifetime. In the years since her death, however, Chopin has been recognized as a leading author of her generation who captured with a visionary intensity the lives of Southern women, often of diverse or indeterminate racial background.

A Note from the Publisher

Spanning many genres, from non-fiction essays to literature classics to children's books and lyric poetry, Mint Edition books showcase the master works of our time in a modern new package. The text is freshly typeset, is clean and easy to read, and features a new note about the author in each volume. Many books also include exclusive new introductory material. Every book boasts a striking new cover, which makes it as appropriate for collecting as it is for gift giving. Mint Edition books are only printed when a reader orders them, so natural resources are not wasted. We're proud that our books are never manufactured in excess and exist only in the exact quantity they need to be read and enjoyed. To learn more and view our library, go to minteditionbooks.com